*"You _____
you, Rob Malcolm?"*

"Some things," she answered, meeting Jed's eyes. Now, with the darkening storm outside, they were the rich color of whiskey.

He leaned forward, looking closely at her. "Like what? What frightens you?"

To let anyone get past the wall that kept her safe, past her tough I-can-do-anything stance. But she wasn't going to tell him that. Still she answered as honestly as she could. "Like trying to be what I'm not."

"And what are you?"

"A ranch woman. A simple unsophisticated ranch woman."

He shook his head and moved closer. "No," he said slowly, "I don't think so. I think you're Snow White waiting to be awakened. Or one of those cacti out there, rough, prickly—but beautiful when it's finally in bloom. You may not know it, Rob, but I do. Your body holds a promise."

Dear Reader,

When two people fall in love, the world is suddenly new and exciting, and it's that same excitement we bring to you in Silhouette Intimate Moments. These are stories with scope, with grandeur. The characters lead the lives we all dream of, and everything they do reflects the wonder of being in love.

Longer and more sensuous than most romances, Silhouette Intimate Moments novels take you away from everyday life and let you share the magic of love. Adventure, glamour, drama, even suspense— these are the passwords that let you into a world where love has a power beyond the ordinary, where the best authors in the field today create stories of love and commitment that will stay with you always.

In coming months look for novels by your favorite authors: Maura Seger, Parris Afton Bonds, Linda Howard and Nora Roberts, to name just a few. And whenever you buy books, look for all the Silhouette Intimate Moments, love stories *for* today's women *by* today's women.

Leslie J. Wainger
Senior Editor
Silhouette Books

Parris Afton Bonds

That Malcolm Girl

Silhouette Intimate Moments

Published by Silhouette Books New York

America's Publisher of Contemporary Romance

SILHOUETTE BOOKS
300 East 42nd St., New York, N.Y. 10017

ISBN: 0-373-07253-8

First Silhouette Books printing September 1988

Printed in the U.S.A.

Books by Parris Afton Bonds

Silhouette Intimate Moments

Wind Song #5
Widow Woman #41
Spinster's Song #77
Midsummer Midnight #113
Man for Hire #153
Wanted Woman #189
Renegade Man #218
That McKenna Woman #241
That Malcolm Girl #253

Silhouette Romance

Made for Each Other #70
Run to Me #526

*Mescalero trilogy

PARRIS AFTON BONDS

has been writing since she was six, though she didn't turn professional until her family moved to Mexico. She gives the credit for her several literary awards to her husband and sons, who have given unstintingly of their love and support.

For Joan Hohl, Gayle Link and Kathic Seidick
All for one and one for all
Can't beat friends like this!

Chapter 1

She didn't like him.

It didn't matter what her sister-in-law had to say about him. She still didn't like Jed Pulaski. The worst part of it was, it looked as if she were going to have to put up with him. Her dream depended on him—and that other man, the one who was talking, the producer, Peter Maxwell. Smooth as churned butter. But Jed Pulaski said nothing. Just listened. Watched.

Tom did that, too. Listened and watched. But her brother's eyes didn't have that look in them, as if he were snarling, way back in his mind. True, Tom and Jed Pulaski both had noses that looked as if a bronc had stomped them, and both had mouths that were always slightly upturned in a faint smile, and a bull-like set to their shoulders, but that was all they had in common.

Jed Pulaski reminded her of a coyote. No, she liked coyotes. Sometimes, on lonely nights, she felt as if they were her companions. The director, or writer, or whatever he was, reminded her more of a wild dog. You would get thinking you could tame it; then all of a sudden, it would turn on you.

He did it now. Turn on her, that is. He startled her so badly that she almost dropped her salad fork. At least she hoped it was her salad fork. She had watched to see which one Marianna picked up. Her sister-in-law always knew the right thing to do.

Rob stared down at the man. His lids were lazy, his mouth curved in that eternal half smile—most likely due to the small, puckered scar that disrupted the clean line of his upper lip. But it was the look in his eyes that got her. It reminded her in a way of the weekend ritual at the Border Bluff Trading Post.

Come Saturday afternoon, the whole territory would begin sprucing up for the *baile*, the weekly dance. Cowboys and vaqueros, roughnecks and railroad men, miners and even border patrolmen, turned out for the dance. And, of course, ranching families from all over the area where New Mexico, Texas and old Mexico came together. With scorn, she would watch the *paseo*—that Hispanic tradition of scouting out the opposite sex. The unattached young men ambled in one direction around the battle-scarred adobe trading post, the young women in the other. If any of them was given the eye and the interest seemed to be mutual, on the next trip around a few words might be exchanged. This could lead to a dance. Maybe even a date. The sidelong glance was known, in both English and Spanish, as the *stolen look*.

But there was nothing secretive about the glance Jed Pulaski was giving her. He looked her over openly, the way a man looks over a filly he's thinking about buying—lids at half-mast to concentrate the glance on the subject of interest. Painters did that. She'd watched Marianna's daughter sketch with her eyes half closed.

Rob was used to being stared at. Why not, as tall as she was? She had always been tall and skinny. Although now, at twenty-seven, she had breasts, and she sure couldn't see what was so damned interesting about the things. Of course, if you were a calf, you would naturally have a hankering for them. But grown men?

After receiving her first interested glance from a roving cowboy, she didn't have to fret herself about being pestered again. It wasn't just that she was a Malcolm, from a fifth-generation ranching family that was one of the most prominent in that part of New Mexico, as well as the Southwest. No, it was something more. Most likely it was the macho idea that cowboys got in their heads—that a woman who raised, broke and trained cutting horses had to be half man herself to succeed.

Marianna had been wide-eyed when she had first come up against Rob and her less-than-feminine ways, but her sister-in-law should have realized that from the time she was three she had grown up motherless and surrounded by men: her father, long dead; her brother Tom; her nephews Colt and Rand; the old Indian Red Eye; the occasional convict working off his time in the Mescalero's service-duty program; and, of course, all the ranch hands who had come and gone. Grumbling Emmitt was the only hired man left from the old days who still rode the ninety sections that comprised the Mescalero Cattle Company's holdings.

The male preoccupation with sex amused her. It had taken all of the six years that Marianna and Tom had been married for Rob to lose her scorn for the softer, feminine type of woman that her sister-in-law personified. Marianna had made her see that feminine women could be courageous, could be strong—though in a different way. Still, the former actress represented a strange breed that Rob could never understand, only fondly indulge.

What did put Rob off was Jed Pulaski's prolonged stare. One glance at an interested cowhand and the man would back off, dismissing her as if she were just one of the boys, which was fine by her. But this ornery man...his gaze challenged hers, and he kept looking, as if he were trying to figure out just what kind of critter she was.

When she had first met him, out on the veranda, she'd been unimpressed, despite his expensive suede jacket, which was at odds with his faded jeans and his beat-up tennis shoes. Marianna claimed that he was the best screenwriter and director to hit Hollywood in decades, that he was— How had she put it? Sort of like the lodestar for some movement or other. A maverick.

He didn't look much like a writer. Rob had been expecting spectacles, sloped shoulders, office-pale skin. Instead, his hair was like scorched gold, longish and curling at his thick, muscular neck. That was another thing. She had this idea that writers were . . . oh, scrawny and stooped. But this man was powerfully built, though he wasn't any taller than her own six feet. And his muscles were subtler, not as obvious as Tom's.

With furtive, sidelong glances, she assessed him from across the table. How could anyone be so tough and so elegant at the same time? The lines at the corners of his eyes said he had to be past thirty. He had a broad, seasoned face, with eyebrows that hitched up high at the outer edges, then sloped sharply down. She supposed most women would have called it a handsome face. Well, it wasn't hard to look at, but it didn't fool her, either.

It was his amber eyes that persuaded her not to dismiss him lightly. Like splinters of yellow-brown light, they gave her a shivery feeling, as if they could look right inside her and pull the soul out of her. As if he could read her thoughts, even the ones that weren't so nice. Especially the ones that weren't so nice.

She shifted in her chair. Mighty uncomfortable things, chairs, if you had to sit in them for more than an hour. Now a saddle, especially a deep Spanish saddle...

"...can build a set on Mescalero's Cinnabar Creek section, and with El Paso only thirty-eight miles away from the line shacks there, you've got a horde of non-union extras to draw from."

Marianna was speaking softly, easily, but with an authoritativeness that indicated that she knew what she was talking about. "*Sierra Sundown*'s cast and crew can either board in El Paso or here at the ranch headquarters. Between the bunkhouses and the extra rooms here in the main house, we can accommodate up to two dozen people, as well as provide the offices the production staff will need during filming."

Peter Maxwell grunted noncommittally. He was a big, silver-haired man, wearing what looked like an expensive, handtailored suit. "What about food services, Marianna?" He went through the ritual of tapping his pipe, then lighting it. Cat-and-mouse ritual, Rob called it. Or hide-and-seek. The producer was delaying as long as possible before revealing his position.

But Marianna was equal to him. Rob had to admit that her sophisticated sister-in-law, still beautiful at forty, could achieve whatever she set her sights on, using her femininity—softly, subtly. Rob had been used to riding herd on all the men on the ranch, and it had taken a while for her to let Marianna help, hazing the men in the right direction in her own distinctly feminine way.

"Several catering companies out of El Paso can provide on-site prepared food and beverages, Peter," Marianna was saying. "And Mescalero has its own chef here to serve full-course dinners to our guests."

Most of the time, the guests were what Rand called "weekend warriors"—arrowhead hunters, anthropologists, writers doing research, treasure hunters and other city slickers. Their foraging was limited to those sections where the cattle weren't pastured. The income from the guest-ranch operations—Marianna's idea—had put the Mescalero Cattle Company back into the black. She had rescued the big, rambling stucco-and-tile house from the last stages of disintegration and converted it into a gleaming showplace, with vases of desert wildflowers everywhere.

She had also begun to promote Mescalero as a film location. Acting as an independent consultant, she had managed to draw several independent producers doing documentaries, but Maxwell-Metro Productions was the first major outfit to show an interest.

"What about livestock, Mr. Malcolm?" Peter Maxwell asked. "The script calls for cattle, horses, chickens."

Tom settled back in his chair and pulled a cigar from the pocket of his leather vest. He was generally content to let Marianna run this end of the business, but he was more than willing to step in when necessary—even if only to steer people in the right direction. "Well, now, that's my sister's department. Rob will ramrod the wranglers and the livestock."

"All but the rogue horse." Jed's keen gaze fastened on Rob. "I've found the horse I want for the star role—on the Doyle Reese spread."

"Doyle Reese?" Her lips tilted downward. "The man's a killer."

Peter Maxwell chuckled. "I don't care if he's Jack the Ripper if he has the—"

"That's not what Rob means," Colt said. Maybe it was his Indian blood, the Apache half of him, but her nephew didn't often volunteer speech. She often wondered how he'd managed to pass his freshman courses at New Mexico State. "A killer is a man who attends the horse auctions," he explained. "He buys up the animals that are left and sells them to the dog-food factory."

"A dirty job," Peter said, drawing on his pipe, "but someone has to do it."

"Not the way he does!" Shyloh's outburst surprised Rob as much as it did the rest of the Malcolm family. Marianna's fifteen-year-old daughter from her first marriage usually fitted Colt's nickname for her— "Shy." Now the girl turned wide, pleading dark brown eyes on Rob. Rob had never been able to resist Shyloh. Buffalo Gal, she called her, because of her unruly mop of moonlight hair. Rob always felt as if they were both outcasts of a sort.

"What Shyloh means," she told Maxwell and Pulaski, "is that a killer goes about his business in a nasty way. There are usually more horses than buyers, and lots of beautiful colts get left. The killer doesn't care what condition they're in. He gets paid by the load. Maybe fifty or more horses crammed in a double-deck semi built with low ceilings for cattle. Colts, stallions, mares—it doesn't matter. They stumble all over each other in boarding, screaming. Then the killer rams his cattle prods between the railings to pack them in tighter. And there's not a damned thing the horses can do."

"That's a touching story," Peter Maxwell said, dabbing at his mouth with his linen napkin, "but we're hiring the horse to work for us, not the man."

"Humane Society regulations require the owner or guardian to be on the set with the animal," Marianna said, her fingers steepled. How could anyone so dainty be so businesslike? Rob wondered. "As much as the Mescalero Cattle Company would like to go to contract with Maxwell-Metro Productions, Peter, I'd have to have your guarantee that Doyle Reese would keep out of trouble while on our ranch."

Which would be like guaranteeing that it would rain in July, Rob thought. Doyle and his brother Cal, the county sheriff, had long held a grudge against the Malcolms. Years before, Tom had bought up a part of the Reese ranch that had gone on the auction block because of poor management, and the Reeses had taken it as a personal insult, one they had never forgotten.

"I'll take care of Reese," Jed said, rising. "Now I'd like to see the Cinnabar Creek site."

* * *

Jed could have ridden in Maxwell's rented limo, along with Marianna and her husband. He probably should have. He had admired the lovely actress—and her work—for years. As far back as twenty years ago, when she'd been just a starlet and he'd been just a punk kid sneaking in off the snow-whipped streets of Pittsburgh's decaying Hill District neighborhood to keep warm in its shabby movie houses. Later on, as a raw young sailor off duty, he'd escaped in the movies when his world had been closing in on him.

So why had he chosen to ride out to Cinnabar Creek in a battered, mud-splattered Dodge pickup instead? One that carried a Winchester .30-30 on the rifle rack above the seat? Maybe it was because he was tired of talking business. Maybe it was because he knew the young woman driving wouldn't be hoping he'd make a pass. She was a no-nonsense type who, he suspected, didn't have the slightest clue about her sexuality.

At first sight, he had mistaken her for a man, what with her plaid woolen jacket over shapeless bibbed jeans, wide-brimmed slouch hat and heavy, dusty boots. Though she was exceptionally tall, she nevertheless moved with an untutored grace. Her brother's light hazel eyes, with their direct scrutiny, looked out of a face characterized by prominent cheekbones and a strong jawline. On her brother, the features were powerful. On her, they seemed set in rigid lines of hauteur, made more noticeable because her dark brown hair was pulled back into a single braid that hung almost to her waist.

Initially, her voice had seemed unpleasant—clipped, commanding, colored by colloquialisms—but it had fallen into perspective with the rest of her, making it natural and expected. She was, after all, a princess of her own domain, of lands ruled by generations of her family, doing what she loved. She had a regal air about her, the straight, firm line of her mouth and the almost belligerent thrust of her cleft chin reflecting pride and self-confidence.

He watched her flick on the pickup's heater. Despite the desertlike landscape and blinding sunlight, the late-March afternoon was blustery and cold. She obviously spent a lot of time in the sun. Her skin had a smooth, toasted sheen. Her hands were scarred, though, from hard work, the nails bitten short.

"You don't like to talk much, do you?" he asked.

She didn't look at him. "Not till I've got something to say."

He grunted. He should have driven out in his Porsche. "How do you feel about all the strangers coming and going on the ranch?"

She glanced pointedly at him. "I feel fenced in. Too many people with too much to say."

He could tell she didn't think much of him. "Don't you ever long to see more of the world than this?" His hand swept the colorless, bleak landscape. He was reminded of Georgia O'Keefe's paintings. Stark, brooding crosses. Stones, weathered and smooth.

Bleached bones and vibrant desert flowers. Paintings symbolizing life, death, eternity and, of course, sex.

"Why should I? Everything that is beautiful to me is right here at Mescalero."

"Beautiful?" His derisive gaze swept the arroyo-scarred land, with its warty blemishes of creosote bush.

"Once you've seen all of Mescalero," she said confidently, "it will itch you the rest of your life. The distance sort of gets into your soul and makes you feel you're too big inside."

He raised one brow. Obviously there were two different points of view here. To him, the land was barren and so full of silence that there was no room for sound.

And the people? He reflected on the ones who had been gathered around the family dinner table this afternoon. Marianna was the only one who could be called beautiful. And perhaps her daughter, though in a lost, waiflike way. The others had seen plenty of wear and tear. Hard-bitten, and as tough as old boot leather. And the old Indian, Red Eye, who looked as if that were about all he drank. A true relic, consumed by the white man's firewater.

Ahead, a dust devil skipped across the caliche road to whirl silently over the desert floor, and she said quietly, "I want to be like that dust, haunting the places I love after I die."

Out of habit, as he did whenever he was weary or had something to resolve, he rubbed the bridge of his nose, which had been broken more times than he could count. "That must be a peaceful feeling, to know where you belong."

She looked at him. "You don't have a place?"

"Not a permanent one," he said. "But if I ever feel the insane need to put down roots, it's certainly not going to be here in this godforsaken wilderness, without a glimmer of intellectual stimulation."

Of course, he'd been raised in a big city that didn't have much in the way of intellectual stimulation, either, at least not in his ghetto. But there had come a day when he couldn't get enough book learning, when the navy had offered freedom and a paid education. He had been a young man dying of thirst and suddenly crawling over the next dune to confront an oasis of shimmering water.

"When I die and go to hell, this place is going to look awfully familiar."

He could tell she resented his words, but he'd long ago stopped offering empty phrases.

"You look tired," she said flatly, tugging her hat lower over her eyes. Apparently she didn't bother with empty phrases, either.

"I burn my candle at both ends." When he saw that she didn't look satisfied by that, he said, "Too much time on the road." And he still had to haul the cast and crew to Mexico in the middle of production to shoot around Tor O'Donnel, who would be absent for two weeks taping a television special.

Rob directed a puzzled glance at his battered hands. "Don't push the pen around much, do you?"

He chuckled. "The Academy would probably agree with you."

"Academy?"

"Of Motion Picture Arts and Sciences. Sort of a club, like the 4-H or the Future Farmers of America. They look upon me as an upstart. A renegade."

She eyed him speculatively. "That the same as a wild dog?"

It was too hard to follow her line of thinking, so he didn't bother. He was wiped out from jet lag. The flight from Orly had been a rough one. Instead he changed the subject and said, "That's some hat you're sporting there."

He hadn't exactly meant it as a compliment, but she astonished him by sliding him a grin from beneath its brim. Almost coquettish, though he was certain she didn't even know what the word meant. It was a sassy, saucy grin.

"Come summer, if you don't have a hat, you'll be able to fry your brain on a barn. This hat—" she touched the brim "—is sort of special. I took a lot of time shaping it over steaming water. It's sort of a disguise, telling some things about me, but hiding other things."

He couldn't imagine her doing anything so heinous that she'd need to hide it. "I suppose the vulture feather stuck in the snake band is symbolic of something?"

She looked away from him, her lips pressed together. "Nope. I just like it."

She didn't say another word after that. Had she thought he was making fun of her? He hoped not. If he had to be stuck out here for three months, he would much rather converse with her than that pompous idiot Maxwell, or one of the airhead starlets he would be directing. Rob Malcolm was interesting, to say the least.

"There it is."

She stopped the pickup and pointed toward a long, low mesa. At its base was a line shack, an abandoned baked-adobe shell. The mesquite fencing that looked ready to collapse at the first hint of a strong wind, the tumbleweeds piled around pockmarked stucco walls . . . to him the place resembled a pigsty. Clustered around it were ramshackle corrals that had been assaulted by the wind and sand and sun. Beyond, in the distance, lay the purple shadows of the Rockies.

"Perfect," he breathed. He was glad they'd reached the film site ahead of the limo, before Maxwell could spoil the setting. The crystal air of the desert, its mountains looming with sharp outlines and clear detail, would serve as a foil for the film's brooding overtone.

"This is nothing," she said, leaning forward on the steering wheel. "My place has—"

"Your place?"

"I have thirty sections of my own." She flashed him a defiant look. "But no one goes there except me and mine."

A curious statement, but she held up a silencing hand before he could comment on it. Across the track in front of them wandered half a dozen antelope. Stately. Graceful. They froze, heads high. Then, farther on, he spotted three coyotes, tails down, circling the antelope. Were the coyotes trying to separate one from the rest?

Beside him, Rob Malcolm quietly plucked the rifle from its rack and slid out of the pickup. He did the same. The southwest wind freeze-dried his skin, drawing all the moisture from it. He walked around the front of the Dodge to join Rob as she moved stealthily closer for a better shot. She raised the Winchester to her shoulder, aimed at the nearest coyote...waited...then lowered the rifle.

He'd seen that happen in navy combat training. Buck fever, they'd called it then. Unable to shoot when the moment came. Not him. He'd been a streetwise kid. If not, he never would have survived. With a grunt, he took the rifle from her slack hands and brought it up to his shoulder.

Before he could pull the trigger, she shoved his shoulder, crying, "No!"

Her thrust was powerful, and he staggered. Without thinking, he swung toward her, grabbed her upper arm with his free hand and shook her. "That was damned stupid. Don't ever do that. Not when some-one's holding a rifle."

She jerked her arm away and glared at him. Be-yond her, the antelope had bounded away and the coyotes had trotted off, bent on other business. "That was a bitch coyote," she snapped. "Maybe carrying a litter. Coyotes don't usually attack healthy animals," she gritted. "Don't you ever shoot one on Mescalero property, you hear—or I'll take this gun to you!"

He stared down at her, amazed. He was good with words, and he said what was on his mind. "You're not big on being a woman, are you?"

Any other female probably would have tried to slap him, or maybe pouted, or even cried, but she laughed. It was a scorching peal of laughter. "This is a man's world, in case you hadn't heard, mister. Now why would I want to live like a woman and have to toady to a man?" She swerved away from him and stalked toward the approaching limo, which kicked up dust that was caught by the wind and whirled away.

"Well, I'll be damned," he muttered.

Rob lay in her bed. Except for the occasional creak of the smoke-darkened vigas, the huge beams that supported the ceiling, the big two-story Territorial-style house was silent. Probably one of the last times it would be for a while. Come May, those movie peo-ple would be arriving. She thought of Jed Pulaski, sleeping in one of the rooms down the hall.

Outside, there was a wolf moon—the orange kind that rises late. It had to be almost two o'clock. Nearby, in the south pasture, several coyotes howled. Their wailing made her shiver. A cascade of sound, wild and ecstatic. Not at all like the quiet, gray creatures they were by daylight.

They always seemed very near, almost beside her, their yellow eyes alert. She'd never been afraid of them.

But she was afraid of Jed Pulaski.

Chapter 2

The first time Rob had mounted Cleopatra's wide back, she had understood what she had been longing for all her life. Rob had always loved horses. Dear old fat Cleopatra had been her first, purchased especially for her by her father.

Then, after her father died, her brother had decided that Cleo was too old for a girl of eight. So Tom had bought Vixen, a quarter horse only two years old and full of fire. The filly had had a fine little muzzle, an arch to her neck and lithe legs that barely seemed to touch the ground, just floated. Tom had left Vixen in the barn until he had had time to break the rebel horse. But Rob would slip into the barn and talk to Vixen and pet her. Then, as the days passed and Vixen settled down, Rob would take the filly out into the corral and lead her around. Not that Vixen had been too pleased with the process.

Rob had a feeling Tom had suspected what she was doing all along, but all he said when he caught her was, "Run the ginger out of her, Rob. It's a damn sight easier on both you and the horse if she runs instead of bucks."

After all these years, Rob still believed the sensation of speed was much more pleasurable on the back of a good horse than in the best racing car. Certainly better than in the red Porsche Jed Pulaski had arrived in. A car merely zoomed on, but on a horse the rider became part of the process, slipped into the rhythm of the animal's movements as if born to do nothing else.

Now she loped Gypsy Belle down the length of the corral, past the stallion barn, preparing to cut a colt from the herd. She barely had to move the reins. Gypsy Belle, wearing the double *M* brand of the Mescalero Malcolms, ducked and dived, lowered her head and went into the herd to drive the calf out.

"Good girl," Rob said.

With the late-May sun beating down on her, she walked the steaming horse over to where Colt stood watching. He said, "That mare will take that fifteen-thousand-dollar cutting-horse purse in Abilene next year."

"She'd better," Rob said, feeling desolation settle over her like an early-morning fog. When she was young, she had barrel-raced in rodeos, and she had been good. But any hope of earning substantial prize money had ebbed with her teenage years, as she had continued to grow taller and taller and taller. Tall girls normally didn't do well in barrel racing, with its tight turns and small, agile horses.

It had taken her a long time to train Gypsy Belle for cutting. A cutting horse was considered the Cadillac of horses for its fluid motion, and Gypsy Belle's pedigree, as long as the Bible's "begats," showed that she was one-hundred-percent cow horse. Gypsy Belle was descended top and bottom from King, the foundation stud of the famous King Ranch and the father of modern cutting.

With Tom owning a little more than three-fourths of Mescalero Cattle Company and herself the other fourth, she often felt that she wasn't doing her share, that her brother had to shoulder too much of the load—making a working cattle spread out of both his portion and hers. So far, her cutting-horse operation had brought in only nickels and dimes. Cutting was a rich man's game.

She desperately needed her own business—and, even more, her own place. She had been irrationally jealous when Marianna had first arrived six years ago as a convict. But as much as she now adored Tom's wife, two women in the same house, regardless of how big it was, could make for strained relationships at times. It was especially difficult for Rob, who was accustomed to running the menfolk.

And now this latest enterprise of Marianna's—opening the ranch house to those movie people. For

the past six weeks, electricians, painters, carpenters
and plumbers had been building the facade of an Old
West town out at Cinnabar Creek, along with an
adobe ranch house, reconstructing the line shack as
part of things. Lately, decorators had been working to
construct the sets where the interior scenes would be
shot. Rob's dark eyebrows, stubbornly flaring at the
outer corners, pulled down in a frown. She would have
to put up with the movie people if she wanted to
achieve her dream.

Her dream of establishing a quarter-horse ranch
where she would both board and train other people's
horses, as well as her own—the kind of operation that
would eventually produce a world champion cutting
horse—would need a lot of work and a lot of money.
With the banks strung out on defaulting oil loans, she
didn't have a chance of obtaining the sizable amount
of financing she'd need that way.

But she'd felt as if she had sold her soul to the devil
when she had agreed to hire out her horses and her
expertise as a stockwoman and work as a stuntwoman on the film. It had probably been a damned
fool thing to do, but at least she would be earning extra money that would go toward covering the cost of
breeding Gypsy Belle to a prizewinning cutting stallion.

"Looks like you've got your work cut out for you,
Rob."

"What?" She turned in the direction her nephew
was staring. Colt always seemed to pick up on things

before anyone else in the Malcolm family did. In the distance, a line of dust marked the route of the caliche road. Definitely more than one car.

Grimly she watched a caravan of vehicles draw nearer. As the vans rumbled past the corral, the names on their sides filled her with an undefinable uneasiness: Saunders Studio Service; The Shotmaker; American Costume Company; Three-Unit Star Hauler.

While the vans, station wagons and trucks drove into the graveled yard, circling like covered wagons at the end of the day's travel, it came to her just what was bothering her—the same feeling she had experienced when Marianna had first arrived at Mescalero. Lovely, feminine, delicate Marianna. Rob had felt as if she had suddenly fallen into water that was over her head and had to fight desperately to reach the surface again.

She hadn't known how to cope, had known only the fear of being ousted from what she was familiar with and understood and loved.

She felt the same way now about all these people arriving from far-flung places. Polished people like Peter Maxwell. Beautiful people like the film's two female stars, Landis Falkenberg and Elise Hyatt. And people like Jed Pulaski, with his hypnotic way of speaking. So different from ornery Emmitt, with his voice that rasped like a blender full of rusty nails. Jed Pulaski was as good with words as she was with her lasso. As good at figuring out people as she was at figuring out horses. With him, she felt exposed.

Somehow, she would have to manage to stay away from him as much as possible.

Ten weeks. That was how long Peter Maxwell had said it would take to complete the filming here at Mescalero, counting the two-week break midway through for shooting at a location in Mexico. Surely she could make it that long. She had to, if she wanted to collect her salary.

As she poured the rest of the tea from the pot into the ceramic pitcher, Shyloh pushed back errant curls from her flushed face. She had tried braiding her unruly hair, as Rob did, but wisps always straggled free. She supposed she would just have to accept that her hair was determined to have its own way and that there was nothing she could do about it. Her mother's natural red hair was just as riotous, but on her the effect was exotic.

"Red Eye! Put that bottle of vanilla back!"

Shyloh turned to see Red Eye standing in the pantry doorway. The old hootch hound, as Rob affectionately called the Mescalero Apache Indian, grinned sheepishly at Haydee. His strong teeth, which gleamed like the silver buttons on his green velveteen shirt, could easily bite the cap off a beer bottle.

Haydee eyed him mercilessly. Marianna had taken her on from UCLA, to earn work-study credits by acting as chef for Mescalero and its guest-ranch operation. The auburn-haired young woman, who was working on a degree in restaurant management, could capably feed a multitude and handle old Red Eye's legendary penchant for drink, and also seemed to be able to handle the infectious smiles and amorous glances bestowed on her by auburn-haired Rand Malcolm. She simply ignored him.

Shyloh could sympathize with Rand. Colt ignored her. He hadn't always. He had been her best friend since the day she'd arrived six years earlier, when she'd been nine. Rand had been her friend, too, but somehow she had always felt closer to Colt. He hadn't teased her when her figure had started developing, as Rand had. "Hunchback," he had jokingly called her after she had taken to rounding her shoulders.

Colt had said nothing, but he must have noticed the change in her. Then he'd gone off to State last year, and whenever he'd come home for holidays he had been distant, unapproachable. He had always been that way to everyone but her, and it hurt her to feel that she'd become just like everybody else. She'd hoped that once he returned for the summer they'd settle into their familiar, comfortable relationship, which rarely needed words.

Haydee frowned at the bony old Indian. "Why don't you crumble the fried bacon? That'll do us more good than you belting vanilla."

He shambled back to the tiled counter, his fierce countenance expressing his discontent. "This one has too much sand!" he muttered. "Damn fine shame!"

Haydee glanced at Shyloh and grinned. The freckles scattered across the young woman's pert nose

seemed almost to twinkle. She reminded Shyloh of a
pixie. "Just what does that mumbo-jumbo mean?"
she asked Shyloh. "Was that a thinly veiled threat? Is
he going to stage a massacre or something?"

"That's a compliment," Shyloh said under her
breath. "Sand is grit. Courage."

Rolling her eyes, Haydee wiped her hands on her
apron and went back to basting the plucked quail
hens. Shyloh picked up a stack of stoneware plates and
entered the dining room to set the table. After school
and during the holidays, she helped out in the large,
remodeled kitchen. As much as she enjoyed working
with Red Eye and Haydee, she yearned to be outside
now that Colt was back home for the summer, wran-
gling livestock for Rob.

"Do be a dear and hook me up."

Shyloh glanced around. Draped over the mahog-
any balustrade was the platinum-haired actress Landis Falkenberg. She had to be nearing fifty, but she
looked much younger. Her career was in its second
spring, and she had become something of a cult figure—and she made sure everyone knew it. Since her
arrival yesterday, along with the other cast members,
she had made continual demands on the household.
Shyloh didn't think the woman had the natural love-
liness of her own mother. Landis Falkenberg
looked . . . well, hard.

She set the plates on the table and went over to the
staircase. The sultry actress had turned her back to
Shyloh and lifted her cascading hair over one arm to

expose the opaline skin where the zipper gaped. Flesh puckered along the edges of the tight bra, Shyloh noted. Hesitantly she climbed the two stairs separating her from the actress.

Landis peered over her shoulder and warned, "Be careful, darling, this is silk."

Shyloh nodded and took hold of the zipper at its base, cautiously inching it upward. The glossy blue material closed snugly, concealing the actress's bare skin.

"Don't be a snail!" Landis shifted her hips, slithering the caressing silk lovingly over her flanks. It was that slight movement that jerked the zipper in Shyloh's fingers upward to pinch a fold of skin. Landis shrieked and whirled. Her palm impacted loudly with Shyloh's cheek. "What the hell!"

Shyloh stumbled backward, almost falling. One hand grabbed at the newel post, the other went to her stinging cheek. The instant contrition in the older woman's eyes didn't diminish Shyloh's humiliation. She spun and fled from the dining room, running blindly down the hallway where she collided with Tor O'Donnel, the film's handsome leading man.

"Hey, what's the problem, sugar?" he asked in surprise.

She pushed past him and out the front door. Instinctively she headed for the place that had become a haven during her years at Mescalero, the two-story gristmill. It didn't matter that the stone structure had crumbled in spots. It was still her fortress, her magical castle, her protection against the pain of growing up. Colt had given her her first tour of the gristmill. Its dust and dimness and musty smell hadn't blighted the aspirations that had flowered there, the dreams of being a renowned artist, of living an exciting life in the exotic places of the world.

Tears in her eyes, she flung herself toward the hay piled in one corner. Instead of soft hay, she collided with something solid and went sprawling. Something metallic pressed against her throat. Dazed, she lifted her head. In the light filtering through the high narrow window, she distinguished her adversary—a saddle. A pile of them lay in front of the hay. She remembered now. Rob had arranged to store the prop company's equine items there.

"Durn her!" she gasped, unconsciously resorting to Rob's slang. Next great, painful sobs began to heave inside her chest, but escaped her lips only in little breathless whimpers. Old leather, saddle oil and horse sweat filled her nostrils with each sharp inhalation.

Light shafted across her, and she blinked at the shadowy figure that emerged from the doorway: a ghost stepping out of the past. Rob had once told her that the Slaughter Mesa line shack on her thirty sections of Mescalero was haunted. Shyloh had liked to believe it, because the source of the superstition was a romantic tale. But the gristmill had no such supernatural background.

The silhouette was of a cowboy, a saddle slung over one shoulder. There was no clink of spurs. Instead, he wore knee-high moccasins. He was built lean and compact, like a mustang, so that his height, only average, wasn't obvious. His copper skin and Indian-black hair shone in the sunlight.

"Colt!" she breathed, the word almost an ecstatic incantation.

He dropped the saddle and hunkered down before her. His long, sensitive fingers cupped her chin and tilted her face to catch the sun's rays. Up close, his eyes weren't really solid black. They were dark brown and velvety, like a horse's.

"What did you run into?" His voice was just as velvety as his eyes.

She shook free of his hand. It made her tingle. "A door."

"Doesn't look like a door print to me."

She could feel her face flushing with color. "Well, it was. I wasn't looking where I was going."

He stared at her intently. "Whenever you're holding back the truth, Shy, I've noticed your eyes glance off to the right while you speak."

Hot tears formed behind her lids. "Just leave me alone."

He didn't. He never took orders from anyone but his father. "Looks mighty like a handprint to me."

The tears trickled over. "That actress...Landis Falkenberg—" she swallowed hard "—I caught her skin when I was zipping her dress for her."

He surprised her by gently wiping the tears from each cheek. His eyes held a tender look, but his mouth was hard. "That actress is a small woman, Shy. Do not spend your emotions for such a poor return."

"Oh, Colt." She slid off the saddles and into the arms that caught her. "I've missed you so!" She liked the feeling of being held by him. That same tingly sensation his hand caused...she could feel it in each of her breasts, where they pressed against his chest. "There was no one to talk to while you were—"

He disengaged her arms from around his shoulders and pushed her away from him. She was surprised by the impatience she saw reflected in his dark face. "You need to find other friends, Shy, more your own age. I won't be around much, except summers."

Something awful was happening, like an earthquake you couldn't feel, even though the layers beneath the earth still separated. That was how she felt. Scared, breathless, awful. She grabbed his hand. "But I don't want other friends. I want you!"

She hated the compassion that filled his eyes. "Look, you're just a child, Shy, and—"

"I'm fifteen! You're only twenty-one."

"There's a world of difference."

Now she knew. It wasn't the earth splitting, it was her heart breaking. "Colt, don't you care about me?"

He glanced off, as if in searching the dark recesses of the mill he might find the right words. "Of course I do. But—"

"It's you who's looking away this time!" she shouted, furious. She felt like a green kid. "You're lying. You don't care about me anymore, do you?"

She didn't want to hear his lies. He had never lied to her before. She pushed past him, out of the gristmill, out into the merciless sunlight that turned beautiful dreams into ugly reality.

"Hello?" Rob released the button on the walkie-talkie. She still didn't feel at ease using the thing.

"Yeah?" the property master answered.

She frowned at the black contraption, then pushed the button again. "For bridles, do you want me to strip them off the saddles or use cavalry bridles?"

"Just go ahead and use cavalry," the prop man said, static making his voice crackle. "Try to use the ones without the cavalry spots on them. You know, the ones that are inconspicuous."

"I got you." She didn't like working for someone else. She'd always been her own boss.

Shoving the walkie-talkie back into its holster on her belt, she strode on over to the corral, where a semi was backed up. In the predawn light, Colt was loading the mounts that were to be used for the first day of production. The call sheet the second-unit director's assistant had given her specified that fifteen horses were to be on location by six that morning, even though set call wasn't until ten.

"Dump the bridles and saddles in the back of the pickup, Colt. Then we'd better head out."

Not that she was in any hurry to reach the Cinnabar section. She'd made it through dinner the evening before, despite being stuck at the same end of the big

T-shaped table as Jed Pulaski. He made her edgy, watching her with those critical eyes the way he did, as if he found something laughable about her. She didn't like being made a fool of. Nettled, she had complained to Marianna later that night, after the cast had turned in.

"What exactly bothers you about him?" Marianna had asked, puzzled.

"He's blunt."

Her sister-in-law had smiled. "So are you, Rob. Look, try to bear with Jed. He might be a little cocky—"

"A lot. Worse than Napoleon, strutting out there in our henhouse."

"I admit that Jed Pulaski's earned a rather reckless reputation as a maverick and that he possesses a Rabelaisian lust for life that—"

"Rabelaisian?"

Marianna had paused, as if deciding what exactly to say. "You might say Jed walks a little on the wild side. Listen, just try and get along with him until the filming is over. You won't be seeing much of him, only occasionally at meals."

The problem was that Marianna could cope with anything. Her feminine way of looking at things didn't hinder her any. As for Rob herself, she wasn't sure she could cope with these outside people. She would be happier than a cat with fresh cream when the filming was over with.

Although the sky was still faintly smudged with stars, people were milling all around the old-time Western set, with its several interlacing streets. For a moment Rob sat behind the wheel and just stared, trying to grapple with all that was happening on the perimeters of the newly created Old West town. Sound trucks and cranes and generator trucks were parked amid the sand and sagebrush.

"La-la Land," Colt commented dryly from his side of the cab.

From beneath the brim of his straw Stetson, he was watching the wardrobe truck. Extras from the area, mostly nearby Deming and El Paso, were lined up— the men at the rear of the big five-ton truck, the women at the door on its side.

Rob recognized a few of the extras from neighboring ranches; some were college kids out of New Mexico State University at Las Cruces. They were dressed in sandals and shorts, sunglasses and baseball caps, tennis shoes and sundresses. A transformation took place after the extras climbed the wooden stairs and entered the truck. They emerged as a bartender, a squaw, a mountain man, a schoolmarm.

The scene, the activity, boggled Rob's mind. Besides the wardrobe truck, there were commissary wagons, a crew van, makeup and rest-room trailers, a prop truck and, of course, dressing rooms for the stars, three to a unit. Her idea of a fairyland began to recede.

A woman in jeans and a T-shirt approached the semi and, shading her face with her hand, stared up at Rob with a frown. "You the ramrod?"

Rob nodded.

"I'm second AD." That meant nothing to Rob, as the woman could apparently tell, because she added, "Second assistant director. I do crowd control, street scenes, things like that. Right now I need ten saddle horses, a buggy horse and two surrey horses down on the set. It's on your call sheet. Exterior scene 145."

"Yeah, right." That was another thing Rob hadn't figured out, the call sheets and all these abbreviations.

"Time to earn the almighty buck," Colt said, and swung down from the cab.

She and Colt backed the horses out of the semi and led them down to the set. Like something out of a surrealist film, the Old West streets were jammed with modern equipment: shiny metallic boards Marianna had called reflector screens; cameras on dollies; generators; boom microphones; and electrical cords that were a tangled mass of black spaghetti.

"Down there," a man with wavy bleached hair said to Rob as he pointed toward one end of the street. "Three saddle horses down there. Two more at the other end. The surrey and buggy horses at opposite sides of the intersection."

"He's probably fourteenth AD," Rob told Colt under her breath. "I'll take care of this street, you take the other."

She mounted Gypsy Belle and, the reins of four of her quarter horses in hand, started off. The trotting horses nervously skirted the film equipment that cluttered the street. Rob didn't have any problem hitching one horse to the buggy. What she had a problem with was the waiting that came afterward. While the production crew worked feverishly to get the set ready, the extras who were already costumed sat in the shade and conversed quietly, read paperback novels or worked crossword puzzles. Others stretched out on the boardwalks and slept.

The desert sun was climbing steadily toward its midmorning position, and the cast had yet to show. Gypsy Belle shifted restlessly beneath Rob. Another hour passed, and Rob swore silently. The movie business sure made poor use of its time. Of course, like the extras, she got paid by the day—for the first ten hours, anyway—so she supposed it didn't matter that much.

At last she spotted Maxwell and Jed Pulaski walking down the main street, deep in conversation. Although Maxwell was big and sleek, Jed Pulaski didn't seem overpowered by the older man. Jed's husky body moved with a tough but easy grace that reminded her of a wild horse—not much to look at when compared to a show animal, but every muscle and bone and sinew was meant for the business of being a horse.

She lost sight of the two men as they moved behind the vans and pickups parked in the street, out of sight of the cameras. At the other end of the street a station wagon, transporting some of the cast from the

Mescalero headquarters, crept over broomweed and scrub brush. Suddenly the rest of the set seemed to come to life. Three extras dressed as cowboys ambled over to her. "AD told us to mount up," one told her.

Remembering the greenhorns in sandals and earrings she'd seen waiting in line at wardrobe, she started to ask if they knew how to ride but decided that was their problem. "They ready to film?"

"Naw," another extra said. "We're just going through rehearsals while the stars are getting made up."

Reluctantly she relinquished Gypsy Belle to one of the "cowboys." From what Marianna had told her, the horses would only be trotted up and down the streets, and there would be no hard riding. Rob didn't want anyone mishandling Gypsy Belle. Come next year, the horse would be the means to achieve her dreams.

A woman in a slat bonnet and a long calico dress, and a man dressed in a waistcoat and a derby, came over to board the buggy. At the far end of the street, another couple took over the surrey. Rob strolled over to the boardwalk to watch from the shade. A unit director in tan trousers was giving some kind of run-through directions to the mounted extras. "Get your driver's position," he told those in the carriages.

For some reason, Rob had the feeling of being watched. Slowly she turned her head to the left, toward the center of town. Jed was pointing her out to the AD with the bleached hair, Jack. As the AD started along the boardwalk toward her, uneasiness stirred in her guts.

"Director wants to see you," Jack told her.

She nodded and followed the AD back. In her own ears, the big rowels of her spurs seemed to clank overloudly against the wooden planks. From beneath her hat brim she could make out Jed, watching her with the intense scrutiny deer hunters used. No, he was watching her with oil-drilling eyes, she decided on second thought. Eyes that drilled right through you.

She could quit now. She didn't have to take this job. But she had never run from anything. Besides, she owed it to Marianna and Tom. In addition, the money would go toward her cutting-horse ranch.

Not far enough, though. And she had the distinctly unpleasant feeling that it wouldn't be nearly enough to make up for working for Jed Pulaski.

"Yes?" she asked when she was standing in front of him. They were at eye level, but she would have sworn he towered over her six feet.

His amber eyes measured her, and she was uncomfortably aware that he missed nothing: her too-long legs, her too-flat chest, her too-wide mouth and her too-pale hazel-green eyes. Lastly they settled on her bib overalls. She was proud of them. They were loose enough that they didn't cut her in half when she sat, and they had plenty of handy pockets. Practical, comfortable and cheap—right out of the army surplus store.

Still, she suspected she had come up lacking in his reckoning. Well, he was nothing but a citified dude. One of those easterners who would never survive in a land like this without the conveniences their money bought them. He was about as useless as one of those actresses. Of course, Marianna had been one of those helpless creatures. She'd been useless, too, at first. But she had proved she had sand by the time Tom had taken her as his wife.

Rob anchored her thumbs in the pockets of her overalls and thrust out her chin belligerently. "You wanted me?"

"She'll do just fine as Tor's stand-in," he told Jack without glancing her way again, dismissing her as if she were no more than a prop, like one of the coatracks or spittoons the set decorator was placing around the set. "As tall as she is, she'll pass for a man easily."

The remark rankled, though for the life of her, she couldn't understand why.

Chapter 3

Spray-paint horses—Great Spirit hot-damn no like,"
old Red Eye declared, his mouth turned down beneath a turned-down nose.

His profile, despite his octogenarian standing, was
noble. Perhaps it was that very accumulation of years
that had made Tom Malcolm give up on reforming the
old Indian, who drank alcohol in all its various
forms—including the native sotol. Red Eye had seen
the white man pass over the land like smoke, had
drunk his way to hell and back after the death of Ellie
Malcolm, Tom and Rob's grandmother, and was still
around to raise more hell whenever the notion came
upon him.

"It sure isn't natural," Rob said, "but if Jed Pulaski says to paint our black horses brown, we paint them brown."

The director or writer or whatever he was didn't want any horses distracting attention from Death Threat, a stallion as black as they came. The man had a hell-for-leather style that annoyed her. She didn't share everyone else's fascination with him. And she wasn't looking forward to this afternoon, when shooting resumed and she began work as a stand-in. That would put her too close to him.

Her can of spray paint began to sputter. "War paint would work better," she muttered in disgust.

"Damn fine shame," Red Eye said again, shaking his head, with its straggly white mane. "More paint in tack room."

With a sigh of agreement, she sent him to the tack room for more paint and picked up his half-empty spray can. The wind had come up, as it always did with the afternoon's thermals, and cocoa-colored paint flecked her hands, throat and face. "Whoa, there, gal," she told the prancing horse, who didn't like being painted any more than Rob liked painting her. "You'll look spiffy as a sorrel, I swear."

From the corner of her eye she spotted Elise Hyatt, strolling down from the veranda porch to watch her. The actress was dressed in a baby-blue T-shirt and jeans that showed her hourglass curves, and her ebony hair was fixed in dog-ears. Rob thought she looked like a ranch girl who had never done a lick of work. And there was no such animal.

"Hi," Elise said, propping her arms on the corral's top railing.

"Hi." Rob continued to spray the mare.

Elise cleared her throat. "Uh, can you tell me where any action is around here?"

Rob paused and glanced up. "Action?"

"You know, dancing, drinking, that kind of thing."

Rob went back to spraying. "We have dancing Saturday nights at the trading post, but that's it."

Elise sighed. "God, it's boring here. And ugly. I've had nightmares that looked better than this."

Ugly? Rob glanced around. Why, at this time of year, the land was positively beautiful. White daisies and cowslips and star lilies covered the ground, reminding her of childhood and fairies. Ground squirrels, their cheeks fat with piñons, darted across the yard. Down by the arena, a yucca stalk was crowned with creamy blooms.

Realizing that Red Eye should have returned with another can of spray paint by this time, she told the actress, "Sorry, but I don't have time to chew the fat with you."

Leaving the young woman looking a little miffed, Rob headed toward the barn. Her suspicions were confirmed: Red Eye sat on his haunches, his back propped against a stall door, a bottle tipped to his mouth.

"You old boozehound!" she said, her fists planted on her hips.

At the sound of her voice, his Adam's apple bobbled rapidly. "Sacred water," he gasped, his rheumy eyes watering at the raw sting of the Jack Daniel's.

"It's spirit water, all right," she said, jerking the bottle from his gnarled hands before he could protest, "but it sure isn't sacred." Wondering just how many more bottles he had hidden in the barn, she poured the whiskey into the sawdust.

Red Eye groaned and threw up his hands. "Now you done it! You gone and angered hot-damn Great Spirit."

She rolled her eyes. "Why don't you go help Haydee with lunch?"

No telling where Red Eye had gotten the whiskey. Indians, oil crews, all manner of people came and went on Mescalero land, and Red Eye seemed to know where they were at all times. And with the film crew here, he had easy access to the booze. After the old Indian left, Rob began to search the barn for any more hidden bottles. Then a disturbance in one of the far stalls drew her in that direction.

Death Threat, who was to be kept at Mescalero until filming was finished, tossed his head and eyed her with a mean, wild-eyed look. She knew that she was soon going to have to begin working with the horse so that they could come to terms before filming the stallion's scenes, but right now her attention was needed elsewhere.

Just as she had expected, Lady Lightning was down, lying on her side with her ribs heaving and her neck arched. Rob had been making routine checks for several days now, ever since the pregnant mare had become restless and begun pawing a hole in her bedding.

"Come up to your time, Lady?" she asked, slipping inside the stall to kneel beside the horse.

A brief inspection confirmed that the delivery would most likely be a normal one. She left to get a plastic bucket of warm water and some antiseptic lubricant, then sat down against the stall wall to wait out the delivery. The mare kept tossing her head and biting at her flanks, and even nipped at Rob a few times.

After a while she heard someone come into the barn. She was expecting to hear Shyloh summoning her to lunch. Instead, she glanced up to see Jed Pulaski.

"I was wondering why that horse out in the corral was half-black and half-brown."

"Sorrel," she corrected. She couldn't figure out just why, but the man made her feel . . . uneasy.

A grin tugged at the scar on his upper lip. "Some easterners—the city slickers, at least—don't have much to do with horses."

She suspected he was poking fun at her. "I had to quit spray-painting." She glanced at the mare, who was panting heavily. "It's Lady Lightning's time."

He pushed open the stall door and hunkered down beside her. "Are you expecting any difficulty?"

"Nope. I just want to be here for the foal. Bonding's important."

"Bonding?"

"A horse-breeding term," she said evasively. Jed Pulaski was so broad shouldered, so powerfully built, that she felt suddenly unsure of herself. Strange, because Tom was a muscular man himself, and taller. "Where'd you get that scar?" she blurted. "The one on your lip."

He fingered it lightly. "I almost forget it's there, except when I'm shaving and nick it. Got it boxing."

"That explains it."

"Explains what?"

Inexplicably flustered, she shifted and refocused her attention on the mare. "Oh, your build," she said vaguely.

"Got started in the navy. I won quite a few fights, but killing wasn't in my soul."

Her glance ricocheted back to him. "Killing?"

His thick brows lowered over eyes that weren't brown, but weren't gold, either. Something like a coyote's when the sunlight struck them a certain way. Except there wasn't any sunlight in the stall. "Men die in the ring, you know." He shrugged those broad shoulders. "But then, they die on the streets just as easily."

He was from the tough east; she supposed she should have expected his indifference. "I don't hold with killing."

His lips drew apart in a smile that said he knew all about her. "You almost killed that coyote a couple of months back."

So *he* remembered that afternoon, too. She hadn't been able to get it out of her mind. Or him. He was so different. "To keep it from killing. And I didn't want to. You would have killed it without giving it another thought!"

He withdrew a cigarette package from the pocket of his expensive shirt, which was striped and made of a soft, polished material. The sleeves were rolled to just below his elbows, revealing the dark hair that matted his forearms. He lighted a cigarette, his hands cupping his gold lighter. All the while, he studied her.

"Something wrong with me?" she snapped.

"Yes," he drawled, exhaling a stream of smoke. "A lot. To begin with, your shoulders are too wide for your hips. Your jaw is too strong. Your eyebrows are too straight. They should wing to conform to your eyes. But it all works."

She wasn't sure if he approved or not, but she couldn't let herself fret if he didn't. Not that she would, because by that time Lady Lightning was stretched out on the hay, pushing hard. A translucent sac appeared, with a little hoof inside. Quickly Rob scrambled to the mare's side. A muzzle came into view, and soon the entire foal began to emerge. Rob knelt and scooped the fuzzy lump against her. Its four skinny grasshopper legs stuck out in all directions.

Within minutes the mare was licking the newborn filly's shiny coat. A new palomino filly, half Arab, half American quarter horse. After several unsuccessful attempts, the foal managed to get to its wobbly feet. Its legs were splayed out in all directions. It tottered a moment, but right away its front legs collapsed.

"Is it all right?" Jed Pulaski asked behind her.

"It's fine." She felt herself grinning foolishly. Birthing always did that to her. "Just trying to figure out where everything goes."

Taking hold of the foal's head, she breathed into his nostrils. "You're mine now, aren't you, little girl?"

When she let go, the filly reached out and nuzzled her cheek curiously. Rob didn't move a muscle, but let the filly discover her face and neck, sniffing her all over, as far as its baby neck would reach. Its breath was warm and moist and tickly.

"So that's bonding."

He was so close that she could feel his breath against her neck. She shivered, shaking deep inside, like a scared horse. She peeked over her shoulder at him. "Yeah. Making sure the foal knows it belongs to you."

"You belong to anyone?"

She pulled her gaze away. His way of speaking was so...so relaxing, as soothing as a summer's eve and as dark as winter molasses. "I'm my own woman."

* * *

Lunch was a noisy affair. Counting the family, ranch hands, cast and crew, more than thirty people were gathered at the long T-shaped table, a Spanish heirloom prized by Marianna.

She glanced along its length, noting the various relationships that were forming between new people and old. The ranch people...she loved them, their kindness, their resilience. The film people...she understood them all too well. Hungry people. As she had once been. Hungry for things they couldn't even have identified.

Her gaze alighted on Elise Hyatt, the young woman Jed had chosen to play the film's ingenue. The raven-haired actress stared with fascination at Colt Kahze, Marianna's stepson. But then, so did pony-tailed Marcie, the young makeup artist.

Colt was so Indian, so dark and lean, so quiet and dispassionate. Naturally he attracted women. What worried Marianna was the attraction her daughter felt for him. As a child, Shyloh had adored Colt. She had thought that the sunshine peeked through his belly button. How long before the teenage Shyloh awakened to his sexual magnetism? How long before she fully realized that Colt wasn't her brother in any way?

Shyloh was glaring at the two young women sitting on either side of Colt. At the moment, her jealousy was aimed at Elise, who was flirting outrageously with him. He was watching the actress's attempt at coquetry with a sort of bitter amusement.

Marianna's maternal instincts even included Rob.
That morning she had watched her sister-in-law
emerge from the barn with Jed Pulaski, and alarm had
vibrated through her. The man had a flash of bril-
liance, a spark of power, an underlying intensity—and
was notorious for his hard drinking. With luck, one of
the women in the cast or crew would draw his attention and he would stop paying his strange brand of
attention to Rob. Still, she wouldn't take any chances.
She would talk to him after lunch, sound him out.

Jed followed Marianna into her office. It had a
warm, comfortable look without being excessively
feminine. The room was done in browns and oranges,
with floral-patterned upholstery and drapes.

"I converted the office from an unused sitting
room," she explained, offering him a chair across
from a matching settee. She chose to sit there, rather
than behind her desk.

He suspected that the lovely middle-aged woman
was using the pretext of discussing the production with
him to ferret out other information. Well, he would
wait. Prison had taught him a lot about waiting. He
crossed his ankle over one knee and lighted another
cigarette. At this rate, he figured, if drinking didn't do
him in, lung cancer would.

Marianna picked up some notes she had made, then
set them down again. "I don't think I'm fooling you,
Mr. Pulaski."

"Jed." She was a number of years older than he was, but she didn't look it. Ranch life wore well on her.

"Jed, then." All business now, she pushed back her flame-red hair and launched into the real purpose of the meeting. "You have quite a reputation, Jed."

"Do I? What as? A hell-raiser? A notorious boozer? A brawler?"

She shook her head. "No. As a man who relishes adventure, who goes for the rush of adrenaline. A gambler, a sportsman—and a womanizer."

"And the last one bothers you, doesn't it?"

She smiled wryly. "If you were in love with my daughter, I'd tell her to get herself to the nearest nunnery."

He chuckled. "You needn't bother, Marianna. Not for me the tender love story and the happy fade-out. Mine is a skeptical sensibility."

"That's exactly what I'm afraid of. In your scripts, only a thin line separates your heroes from your villains, and love offers no hiding place."

Cigarette smoke curled from the corner of his mouth, which was lifted in a dry smile. "That last sounds like a line from one of my screenplays." He stabbed out his cigarette in a terra-cotta ashtray. "What do you want from me, Marianna?"

She had the grace to glance away, but when she turned her gaze back to him, it was almost pleading. "I don't know, exactly. Maybe that you'll leave the flowers you find here unplucked."

His brow lifted. He thought of Rob Malcolm, with her laissez-faire hair, her infidel style. His bluntness masked his reticence. "I'm not planning on seducing any of your ranch maidens."

"No, but you could lure them away. You have vast reserves of will, or luck, or whatever it is that entices impressionable women."

"I wouldn't lure a woman anywhere," he said flatly, getting to his feet. "I like my women willing and uninterested in commitment. I'm too selfish ever to surrender my freedom. As someone else who has been in prison, you should understand that more than anyone."

Chapter 4

The film company's workdays were long, at least twelve hours. Grudgingly Rob developed a better opinion of the cast and crew during the week that followed. Oh, they might complain about the sand that got into the commissary truck's food trays, the draining heat, the wind, but they stayed with it.

Of course, the weather never bothered her. She was accustomed to hunting stray cattle in stinging blizzards and baling hay under the sizzling summer sun. It was the waiting, the waiting and what seemed like the waste of time, that made her edgy. She was learning that it could take as long as three days to make thirty or forty seconds' worth of film that was acceptable to Jed.

He made her edgy, too. He was demanding, keen-eyed, critical. But the stand-in job, which meant she had to put up with his orders as she took Tor's place while the lighting was set up, brought in more much-needed money, and she couldn't beat that.

"Hold still."

She grimaced at the DP. She was beginning to pick up on all the abbreviations. Marianna had told her that as director of photography the irritating little man had one of the most respected positions in the crew.

"Tilt your head more toward the reflector, sweetie," he told her.

Obligingly she turned her head toward the shiny metallic board while another man held up a light meter to her face to take a reading. The lights and cameras were being set up, the grips were laying the tracks for the camera dolly, and the principal actors were in makeup or studying their lines. Gaffers were repositioning cables around her and hooking up boom microphones and other sound equipment. It all seemed so disorganized to her, but they all appeared to know exactly what they were doing.

She was learning that there were some advantages to being a stand-in. She was considered part of the cast, as opposed to the extras, who were treated like a herd. "That's where the term cattle call came from," Elise had explained, a little impatiently. As part of the cast, Rob got to eat first and choose from the best food. Not for her those Styrofoam boxes holding soggy sandwiches that had been made the day before.

Even though it was evening and the desert air was cool, the powerful carbon arc lights made her perspire. She tried making her mind a blank, the way she did when she rode pasture for hours on end.

This week Jed was shooting all night scenes, which meant no one got back to Mescalero before two in the morning, and that made for short tempers. Jed's seemed to stay that way. Adrenaline ran through his blood like nitro. "All right," he ordered. "First team back in."

Relief surged from her in a sigh. For the moment her work as part of the second team, the stand-ins, was over. Tor O'Donnel, who had been concentrating on his lines, climbed down from his tall canvas chair and handed her his script. He was dressed in a Western shirt, a leather vest and boots. "The man can be a beast, can't he?"

She grinned. "A rabid dog!"

He chuckled, tossed back his longish dark brown hair and sauntered off, murmuring his lines to himself. ". . . all you need is a water hole and a fast gun."

She had taken a liking to the handsome, lanky actor. She hadn't expected to. Not when she'd figured out that to put it plain, he was more likely to show an interest in one of the local cowboys than in one of the cowgirls. He wasn't obvious about it, but growing up on Mescalero, she had learned the importance of watching for the little things: the shift of the wind; a buzzard circling overhead; a pregnant cow with her tail distended, the sign that she was ready to give birth.

That was how she had picked up on Tor, by notic-ing the little mannerisms that most folks missed, at least at first. But he was kind, and smart, too. He took the time to explain a lot of the movie terms to her. Like when she had asked what "atmosphere" meant on the call sheet.

"You know," he had said, his dentist's-dream teeth gleaming. "Cows, horses, Indians, bartenders. Things like that."

Best of all, though, he didn't look on her as an oddity, the way Elise and Landis did. They stared at her as if she were a skunk getting ready to spray. At the moment the two women were doing a scene on the far side of the set, which pleased Rob. The farther away the two city women stayed, the better.

The boom operator lowered the microphone. "Everybody ready to roll, then?" Jed said.

The second assistant cameraman held up a slate marked with the number *41* and clapped it shut.

"Quiet!" Jed called out.

A woman—the script supervisor, Linda—yelled, "Quiet, please!"

"Roll camera, please." That was Jed.

"Rolling!" the woman called.

It was another one of those little things that di-verted Rob's attention, this time from the scene in progress. Or several little things, actually. The white curtain in the second floor window above the saloon was blowing outward. The scent of the air, coming down off the mountains to the west, was another clue, as was the rustling sound of the heavy black plastic that masked the desert landscape behind the facade's open windows and doorways.

If she had learned one thing from that first week of shooting, it was not to interrupt a scene. But another thing she had learned was how expensive it was to rent those costumes, despite the fact that many had frayed hems and cuffs. The wardrobe mistress had told her they cost from five hundred to fifteen hundred each. So she felt obliged to warn of the weather change. "Rain coming!"

Jed's tawny head spun in her direction, his disbelieving eyes leveled on her. "Cut!" he yelled.

For a moment he just stood staring at her, his mouth set in a forbidding line. Charley, one of the special effects people, rolled his eyes. No one dared cross Jed, although Peter Maxwell, who had arranged the film's financing, wasn't above a respectful wrangle with him.

The whole set seemed to go silent, something that rarely happened, even during shooting. Usually all sorts of whispered directions and conversations went on out of boom range. But not now. Now everyone was quiet, all eyes staring at her. She shifted her weight from one boot to the other. The watchful gazes followed Jed as he strode toward her with a seen-it-all casualness.

His narrow-eyed gaze ran over her. Then, hands on hips, he asked softly, "Do you have any idea what it costs to reshoot a take?"

She was used to Tom shouting when he was furious. This quiet anger confused her. She tilted her chin. "More than ruined costumes?"

He expelled a grunt of exasperation. "All right, I'll bite. What are you talking about, Malcolm?"

She wasn't quite sure if he was making fun of her or not, using her surname as if she were just one of the men, but she jerked her chin over her shoulder. "Back there. There's a rainstorm moving in quick." She held out her palm to catch the first sprinkles and arched a mocking brow at him. "See?"

He glanced up. Advance scatterings of black clouds, unnoticed against the darkening sky of evening, had boiled over the Florida Mountains and were streaking across the violet-hued sky. He frowned. "All right," he told everyone. "Break for chow!"

The corners of her long mouth tilted ever so slightly. "Too late."

At that the rain began to fall in earnest. The cast and crew scurried for shelter. Since most of the buildings were only facades, the majority of them were forced to retreat under awnings along the boardwalk, while a few piled into the pickups and vans that were parked along the streets. For a second she stood there, gloating as the street emptied. Rain didn't bother her, though she was no fool when it came to lightning.

She turned to go, but Jed latched on to her wrist. "Come on, Malcolm. You're going with me."

As strong as he was, his grip was surprisingly gentle. She could have yanked free, but she let him tug her along with him, wherever it was he was going. Purposefully she slowed her pace, digging in her heels a little. Let him get as drenched as a cat!

With rain washing over them, he towed her a full block to the edge of the set and the prop company's semi. Its back doors opened onto a broad improvised wooden platform and stairway. Inside, there wasn't that much room. Counters and ceiling-high cabinets ran the length of both sides.

Snatching her hand from his, she wiped the water from her face and eyes. Her gaze avoided the man watching her. Instead, it skittered over the contents of the trailer's various compartments: salt shakers; play money; parasols; wicker baskets; briefcases; purses; guns and gunbelts.

At last she turned her eyes on him. Hips braced against a counter, arms crossed, head canted, he seemed to be studying her, puzzled, reminding her of the way the weekend geologists examined the rare rocks they came across when they stayed at Mescalero.

Prompted by his intense regard, she looked down and noticed that the rain had molded her cotton shirt to her. She sighed, glanced back at him and drawled, "You've never seen teats before, mister?"

Her directness caught most people off balance. They would hem and haw, trying to find words to cover their embarrassment. But he surprised her by chuckling. Someone else might have called the smile that went with the laughter pleasant, but not if they'd looked deeper, to the snarl behind it. "You know, Malcolm, as opposed to animals, human beings—men and women alike—find teats very sensuous."

It was the summer rain, she supposed, making her feel all steamy-hot. It was pouring down heavy enough that it would likely last a long time. She sat on the floor, her back against the cabinet, her arms wrapped around her updrawn knees. "I can't imagine why. Teats is teats."

He pushed wet hair the color of old gold off his forehead. "Perhaps because they feel good, very good, to the touch. You have experienced the pleasure of being touched, haven't you?"

He was laughing at her now. She knew it, even though his expression hadn't changed. He was still smiling that slightly puzzled smile and watching her from beneath half-closed lids. She set her mouth in a grin. "Well, I've always considered animals smarter than humans."

"You're dodging my question, Malcolm. So I'll ask you another that intrigues me even more. Why are you opposed to acting like a woman?"

She cocked her head. "I told you. Besides, women still have to make compromises men don't."

He nodded thoughtfully. He pushed himself away from the counter and sat down on the floor across from her. The space between the two cabinets was tight, and up close she could see that his eyelashes were short and thick, his eyes more gold than brown, with glints of jet. "You don't like the submissiveness that you think comes with being a woman, is that it?"

She stared back at him. "I don't like nosy people."

A muscle twitched near the corner of his mouth again. "Have you ever heard of Hatshepsut?" She blinked, and he said, "No, I thought not. Fifteen hundred years before Christ was born, Egypt's king died and his wife, Queen Hatshepsut, was designated as regent—that is, she was supposed to rule until their son was old enough."

She wondered where all this was leading.

He must have read her thoughts in her expression, because he said, "I'm getting to the point, Malcolm. Hatshepsut refused to let their son rule. She pushed him into the background and proclaimed herself king. In her statues she portrayed herself wearing not only the royal crown but sometimes the royal beard. You see, she wanted to reinforce the concept of a strong ruler. Her plan was to make the succession pass through the queen. It's called matriarchy. But ironically, by assuming the *kingly* attributes of the office, Hatshepsut herself contributed to the continuation of the patriarchy—that is, the royal line would be descended from the king."

She stared out at the curtain of rain that veiled the storefronts and asked casually, "You're saying she should have been strong...as a woman? Shouldn't have tried to act like a man?"

A look of satisfaction eased the lines around his mouth. "You might say that."

She let her own grin widen. "Well, I'd say that she should have been herself."

He stared at her thoughtfully. There was something new in his eyes, though she wasn't exactly sure whether it was respect. It was sort of the way a horse would look at you when it found out it couldn't throw you. "You're not afraid of much, are you, Rob Malcolm?"

"Some things," she answered, meeting his eyes. Now, with the darkening of the storm outside, they were the rich color of the whiskey old Red Eye drank when he could get hold of some.

He leaned forward, really looking at her now. "Like what? What frightens you?"

To let anyone get past the wall that kept her safe, past her tough "I can do anything" stance. But she wasn't going to tell him that. Still, she answered as honestly as she could, because dishonesty wasn't in her. "Like trying to be what I'm not."

"And what are you?"

She paused to think that one over. "A ranch woman. An unfettered ranch woman."

He shook his head. His hair, as it dried, was curling at the neck and ears. "No," he said very slowly, "I don't think so. I think you're Snow White, waiting to be awakened. I think you're one of those cacti out there, rough, prickly—but beautiful when it's finally in bloom. You may not know it, Rob, but I do. Your body holds a promise."

Briskly she wiped her hands together. "I think you talk too much, Mr. Pulaski."

He didn't act put out at all. "Indeed? What else do you think about me?"

She eyed him from beneath her lashes. A trick? She shrugged. He couldn't hurt her. "You talk real nice, but I have an idea you're tough underneath. And maybe a little scared, too."

He did a double take at that. "Scared?"

"You know, like a cornered dog. Or a wolf that's wandered onto a place where humans are living."

A strange mixture of amazement, amusement and irritation sparkled in his eyes. With a natural grace that she supposed came from boxing, he thrust out his legs, one on either side of her. "I take it you don't like wolves?"

"They're loners."

"You might know a lot about coyotes, Malcolm, but you don't know much about wolves. They're one of the few species in the animal kingdom that mate for life. You don't 'mate' a horse, you breed it. Horses don't have that instinct that ties them to one mate until death. Zoologists say that when a wolf's mate dies, the animal grieves, just like a man—or a woman. Tell me, where did you get the name Rob?"

He had thrown her off balance. He'd been telling her something fascinating, and then he'd suddenly switched directions. "It's for Roberta, after my father. What kind of name is Pulaski?"

"Polish. And please, spare me the Polish jokes. Why do you use Rob, instead of Roberta?"

He was doing it again, peeling away little pieces of her armor. She glanced away at the cardboard boxes labeled with the names of the principal actors, then back to his watchful face. She shrugged. "It's shorter."

"You like everything short and direct and simple?"

She wasn't used to all this talking. No one had ever talked this much to her. The men always had too much work to do to bother with conversation. She would have stood up, shifted, paced, but his outstretched legs trapped her. "Yeah," she muttered uneasily. She was getting in over her head, and she knew that he knew it. "No room for misunderstanding."

"Then I'll be direct. I find myself wanting to touch you."

She jerked her head upright, all attention. "Why?"

There was a smile on his lips. It was as if he knew something she didn't. He probably knew a lot. But only about some things, she reminded herself, not everything. "I think I like your way," he said. "Short and to the point. You don't bother to play long-drawn-out games." He folded his arms, as if prepared to wait as long as the storm took to wring itself out. "Well, now, Malcolm, I want to touch you because you're very different, very real. Because your skin holds the warmth of sunshine. Because your eyes hold honesty, your mouth strength." She could feel his gaze traveling over her throat, her eyes, her mouth. "And it holds passion, too, Rob. Have you ever been kissed?"

She stared at his mouth, full and taunting. In the cramped space, she could feel the heat coming off him. It seemed to singe her. "You talk too much," she said crisply, and rose swiftly to her full height.

"I thought not." He came to his feet with her. His eyes laughed at her. "Aren't you even curious?"

They were separated by mere inches, squared off against each other. Overhead, the desert rain drummed its primitive beat. And inside, unseen electrical currents arced between them. "I've never really thought about it one way or the other."

That wasn't wholly the truth. Sometimes, when Marianna would give Tom that long, blistering signal, or when she would intercept the quick, yearning glances Rand flashed at Haydee, she would wonder what was so exciting about sex. There must be something. Mescalero's last convict ranch hand had left to marry widow Ruthie Cuddahay, yet Bronco Bobby had always bragged that he loved all women too much to ever settle for one.

Rob had long ago come to the conclusion that when animals had urges they just took care of them and got on with the business of life. But humans were fools, always pining for love. Yes, animals *were* smarter than humans.

Jed cupped her chin, his thumb finding the soft hollow beneath her lower lip, then gliding over the lip itself before he tilted her chin up. ''Then think about it.''

She could have drawn away, but she watched, eyes wide, as he lowered his head. His mouth hesitated just above hers, in a kiss more of breath than of body. When his lips finally touched hers, her lids slid closed. His mouth slanted over hers, his lips moving back and forth, as her fingers had once slid over Marianna's silk nightgown, just delighting in the touch.

In surprise, she thought how soft and gentle his lips were. There was something soothing in their movement, their pressure on hers. They were warm and moist. She liked the security of his hands gently holding her shoulders, as if he were tempering his strength for her. She liked the feel of his hard body touching hers, all up and down. Never had anyone held her like this.

Something unseen, powerful, dark, stirred beyond her imagination. An answering stirring awoke deep inside her. Way down, tickling, tingling, then changing to a pleasurable ache as his lips changed their pressure... harder, searching, opening. His tongue teased just inside her lips. It was a velvet roughness, a sleek wetness. Flames licked her from the hot cavity of his mouth. She trembled, finding it as hard to stand as if she were a newborn foal.

He raised his head. His breathing was easy, as if nothing had happened. He was watching her through heavy-lidded eyes, gauging her response. ''Well, what did you think about it?''

The heavy sensuality that had brought them together still hung in the air. That feeling of being fettered... She pulled herself out of his arms. Hot shame spilled color into her cheeks. She glared at him. "I think I'm a fool for going along with this. But you're an even worse one, Jed Pulaski. You play at feelings like a cat plays with a ball of yarn, stringing it out, fraying it."

His mouth was tight above his square jaw. In his eyes she saw regret, loneliness.

Then she left him for the cleansing rain. She simply went out in the center of the make-believe street and turned her face up into the needle-sharp droplets that stung her benumbed flesh to life again.

Marianna slid her hands up over Tom's shoulders. Her fingers tangled in the rich silk of his sun-gilded dark hair as her body arched against his driving one. It was incredible, how she could never have enough of him.

"That's it, darlin'," he murmured. "Feel it, feel how good it is."

She grew dizzy. Her breath caught in her throat at the sensation pulsing through her veins. How had she ever thought that she could never be happy on a ranch as large and as isolated as Mescalero, where solitude was a fact of life? And how had a career woman, a professional actress, centered her life around this one man?

Because he had become the sun and she a planet, radiant with his protective light.

Unjustly convicted of dealing in drugs, she had believed her life over... and instead it had only just begun. At Mescalero.

He halted in his stroking, his powerful body supported on the enormous columns of his arms. "Tonight, darlin', I'm going to make a baby in you."

I'm too old, I'm forty, she wanted to protest. *Yet if only...*

There had been just her daughter, Shyloh. She had wanted more children, but perhaps not enough to seek out her former husband's arms. Jax Viking might have been a legendary rock musician pursued by legions of eager women, but he knew nothing about really loving, about giving...as she had discovered as the years had worn on.

Tom dipped his head to suckle at her breast, his mouth hot and wet on its swollen, dusky-tipped peak. She groaned, wanting his body against hers again, a sweet, heavy weight. His large hand burrowed into the riotous red curls tumbling across the pillow. She looped her arms around his neck and buried her face against his hair-matted chest. She wrapped her legs around his hips, and the muscles in his arms knotted.

"Don't stop riding me," she whispered raggedly.

"Hell, darlin'," he exulted with a lazy grin, "I'm just getting out of the gate."

Chapter 5

Jed swirled the Crown Royal in his glass. The Canadian whiskey was a warm, rich color. The same couldn't be said for Rob Malcolm's long hair. It was dark brown. That was all. She was only a tall, whipcord-lean young woman with waist-length dark brown hair. An unfettered ranch woman, she had called herself. But she had left out any mention of her penetrating hazel eyes under slashing eyebrows. Eyes that sparkled with her amazing vitality, that glowed with her intrinsic intelligence, that glittered with challenge.

She knew who she was, and he had to admire that.

He would have bet a case of Crown Royal that she didn't know anything about life's dark alleys. She was intense sunshine and green pastures and desert sands that dueled with the wind, racing just one step ahead. But set her down in one of his back streets, and just how well would she fare then?

An interesting subject for a film.

But he had to get through this film first. *Sierra Sundown* was his soul. He had written it as an allegory...the story of a rogue horse and the cowboy who went rogue with it. His others had been adventure films that had made tidy profits for Peter Maxwell and his investors. He had also reaped a tidy profit for himself. If he would do anything differently, he supposed, it would be to make his money before he spent it.

Nonetheless, he wasn't making this one for profit, though Maxwell, who was all "bottom line," was betting on it. The producer had sharp entrepreneurial instincts. He could meld a handful of outside investors into a unit capable of financing the costliest film. Nothing ever got to the man except red ink on his company's ledger.

Jed had invested a piece of himself in this film. After a decade of directing commercial films, he had laid himself on the line and written *Sierra Sundown*. Its success meant more to him than the movie kingdom would ever understand.

Despite the years he had spent consorting with the denizens of Beverly Hills and Hollywood, his veneer of polish remained only that—a veneer. He still kept his back to the wall. And his back was to the wall on *Sierra Sundown*.

All in all, he was pleased with the casting. Tor O'Donnel, a brooding Shakespearean actor capable of powerful performances, was ideal as the hardworking but restless cowboy combating the elements, the two women in his life, the bankers and, most of all, himself—the man's sexual preferences be damned.

And Landis had the experience to carry off her part. Since she couldn't play the sex goddess forever, she was taking a chance with this film, too, hoping to prove herself as an actress with range. She was abandoning her drop-dead sensual image for that of the hard-bitten ranch wife battling for her husband and their land. She just might succeed in netting herself an Oscar.

What troubled Jed was the ingenue role. Twenty-one-year-old Elise Hyatt was visually perfect for the part of the young, slightly tawdry Gypsy girl of seventeen who flees Mexico to take refuge in a canyon with the wild mustang stallion and his harem of mares.

With her tousled raven-black hair, Elise was just what he had been searching for: a precociously intelligent, sensually provocative yet childishly innocent wild thing. He had thought the task of finding the right ingenue impossible—until her first audition had proven to him that she could act well enough to convince an audience that the rancher would walk away from all that mattered for her and her untamed horses.

Trouble was, Elise admitted that she had no affinity for horses. But she was so damned right for the part that he had decided to work around that by hiring a stuntwoman. Rob Malcolm would double for her in the long shots that required riding bareback and other things Elise couldn't pull off.

He tossed down the rest of the whiskey. He supposed that if he had one regret it was that he hadn't learned to enjoy wine instead of hard liquor. He could select the best wines by vintage and bouquet, but he really didn't give a damn about them one way or the other.

He rose from his bed and crossed to the window, where the house cat, Phrank, sat sunning himself. Outside, the white-painted fences sparkled in the sunlight. It was barely ten o'clock, and that Malcolm girl was in the largest corral, working her horses. Amazing, considering that they hadn't finished filming until two-thirty this morning. By the time they'd reached the ranch house and turned in, it had been almost four. The rest of the house was still asleep. At least the cast and crew were. Tom Malcolm and his ranch hands had already ridden out to God knew where.

He stood watching her, fascinated by her agility, her strength, her self-command. She walked among the horses, apparently talking softly to them, from what he could tell at a distance. Then she wheeled and turned, as quick as that prize cutting horse of hers, using her hands and her quirt to separate the ones she wanted.

She drove one—by God, it was Death Threat—into a pen and then pulled up the gate rails. Doyle Reese had sworn the horse was virtually unmanageable.

Jed's brow arched with respect as he watched her take a rope and throw a loop around the stallion's forefeet with all the skill of a rodeo cowboy. Once she got a hackamore onto Death Threat's head, she hitched him to a post in the middle of the pen and saddled him.

When she untied the horse and reached for a stirrup, the stallion kicked out a hind hoof. She flicked his haunches with her quirt, waited a moment, then mounted. It seemed to Jed that the horse went straight up into the air, wheeling, twisting, spinning. The young woman just sat on him, glued in the saddle, until the horse was lathered around the reins and saddle and walking around the pen instead of diving and bucking.

At last she climbed down and loosened the cinches. From his vantage point he could see that her denim shirt was damp with sweat and clung to her back. She swung the heavy saddle easily over her shoulder and, with her free hand, slipped the hackamore off and started toward the gate. Behind her, Death Threat suddenly charged.

"God almighty!" Jed breathed.

She spun and ducked as the stallion reared. He pawed the air with his forelegs and struck out, catching her on the shoulder. She went down in the dust, but she struck out, too. Her quirt caught the stallion across the chest. His hooves flashed over her and came down just as she rolled away. She lashed out again, this time at his face. The stallion, panicked by the sharp sting of the quirt, whirled and fled to the far side of the pen.

Jed thumped his glass down on the windowsill and rushed from the room, taking the stairs two at a time. By the time he reached the pen, Rob Malcolm was already outside it and brushing the dust off her clothes. The entire back of her shirt was torn away where a hoof had caught the fabric, and blood streaked her skin.

She shook her head, as if to clear it, then looked over her shoulder at the stallion, who was still standing at the far side of the pen and snorting. "That animal is crazier than loco weed."

He almost laughed at the understatement, but she had swung back toward him. Dirt coated one of those full cheekbones. "Come help me."

Bemused, he followed her into the tack room. It smelled of leather and damp wool and horse sweat. She straddled a saddle perched on a two-by-four, her back to him. "There's liniment on the shelf and muslin wrapping in the first-aid box."

He drew his gaze away from the expanse of bare flesh to search the shelf. The liniment and muslin wrapping were where she'd said they would be. "I don't suppose I have to warn you that this is going to sting?"

"Just get on with it," she muttered.

He came up behind her and began to dab at the bloody patch. The gash was deeper than he had thought. Around it, the flesh was rapidly turning blue.

But the rest of her exposed back was startlingly white. Alabaster, he thought, mesmerized. She didn't wear a bra. That said something about her disdain for the rules designed to constrict women.

There was nothing fragile about her bone structure. The supple column of her neck flowed into square, capable shoulders. Her braid followed the lengthy line of her spine. It was straight and strong, in contrast to the soft curve of her waist and the ridges of her shoulder blades, which were smoothed by subtle muscle and tendon. Rodin would have loved sculpting her.

He draped her braid over one shoulder, his fingers lingering at her nape. He was surprised to note the slight trembling of his hand. Too much drink these days?

At his touch, she inhaled sharply. He returned his attention to the gash. As quickly as he wiped it clean, blood seeped back in again. At least the blood wasn't spurting. She winced each time he dabbed at the wound, but made no sound.

She sat with her arms pressed over her chest, wrists crossed just below her neck. The pose whispered of unworldly modesty. He would have expected her to be hardened by life, unabashed by nature's indelicacies.

"A real bronco breaker," he said in an idle tone, "wouldn't let Death Threat get away with that." He wanted to prod her a little, to see just how far she could be pushed before she lost her self-control.

"I don't hold with *breaking* horses, Mr. Pulaski."

He paused in dabbing at the wound. She was staring straight ahead, at the bridles and bits and halters dangling from the wall pegs. "Why's that?"

"'Cause it's just that—breaking them. Oh, I can do it, all right. But it isn't the right way. Breaking a horse takes the spirit out of it—or else turns it ornery and mean."

"Reese must have been trying to break him, then."

She almost snorted. "That animal would stomp the tobacco juice out of Reese quicker than you can spit. You can bet Reese would never forget a run-in with that mustang."

His fingers grazed her purpling, bruised flesh. "I don't think you'll be forgetting the feel of him tap-dancing across your back, either."

She flinched at his touch. "That'll do just fine."

She turned sharply, as if to go, and his fingers trailed over the curve of her shoulder to nestle in the hollow of her collarbone. Her palms, clasped against her chest, held her tattered shirt intact over her small breasts. He had her avenue of escape blocked. He lowered his voice to a casual pitch. "You might let me bandage this before you run away."

Green eyes stared out of a willful face whose sensuality took him by surprise. "I'm not running away. I don't run from anything."

"Really? You never answered my question that rainy afternoon in the prop trailer."

Her eyes narrowed. "What's that?"

"Are you aware of the pleasure of being touched here?" His fingers drifted down to gently brush one breast.

She went still. She smelled of earth and sweat and woman, and the combination inexplicably excited him. It had been a long time since he had been excited simply by a woman's nearness. A long, long time.

Her lids lowered, her sun-tipped lashes fringing her incredibly high cheekbones. Killer cheekbones that would have stopped a thousand "local yokel" jokes in their tracks. Then she raised her lashes and stared openly at him. "Yes."

"Was it enjoyable?"

She shrugged. "I don't remember."

He arched a brow. "You would—if it had been." He tamped down the surge of heat sparking his blood. Unaccountably, he didn't want her to be afraid of him. He stepped back and reached for an adhesive gauze patch. He half expected her to flee, but her eyes followed him with a quizzical expression.

"Turn around," he told her. "And lift your braid out of the way."

She did. His mind's eye framed her pose. She was a natural for the camera. He would have bet his home in Malibu on it. Gingerly he pressed the adhesive strip over her wound. "There. And don't get sick on me. Shooting call's at three this afternoon, and the rehearsal of scene 38 is first up."

Almost aristocratically, she rose, her full height matching his. Her unyielding gaze was leveled on him.

"I'll be there, Mr. Pulaski," she said flatly. "I want that money."

"Why?" She didn't seem like the kind of person to be attracted by the lush green of U.S. printed lettuce.

With a jerk of her head, she tossed her braid back over her shoulder. How would her long, thick hair look spread like a sable mantle around her? She would be a Western version of Lady Godiva. "For what it will buy me. A cutting-horse operation on my own place. Then I won't be beholden to anyone." In the dimness of the tack room, her pale eyes smoldered. "With my own business, I won't have to put up with folks coming and going and asking foolish questions."

He rested his weight on one foot and regarded her. "You know, Malcolm, Oscar Wilde once said that there are really only two tragedies in life: that you might never get the thing you want most, and that you might get it."

If he thought that would impress her, he was mistaken. She considered his statement for a moment, then asked, "Who's this Oscar Wilde fellow?"

"Oscar Wilde, my dear girl, was an Irish novelist and poet. And while I am most decidedly Polish, I find we have certain things in common—our appreciation of beauty, for instance." He decided to test her, perhaps even shock her, and added, "And, of course, we both did time in prison."

Her eyes dilated. "What for?"

"Well, you'll have to read up on him to find out what he did, won't you?"

Her mouth stretched in an exasperated line. "No, *you*, I mean."

"I don't know if I want to tell you about me. Oscar Wilde's story is so much more interesting."

"Well, I'm not interested in either of you!" she retorted.

At that, he erupted in delighted laughter. Another mistake, because it only drove her away. Beguiled, he stared after her as she stomped out of the barn.

Death Threat had a different line to him than her quarter horses—he was pure mustang all the way through. All iron and guts and shaped like a barb, without even a smattering of white on his legs. He had the look of being strong and solid with a sleek ranginess about him. But he sure wasn't range gentle.

Rob studied the stallion as he stood on the ridge, tossing his head and drinking in the wind. His every movement seemed to indicate his disdain for burly Doyle Reese, who held the rope around his neck. Reese was a heavy, balding, surly-faced man, though he had once been good-looking.

Nearby, the crew assembled reflectors and sound equipment. A pickup carrying a generator slowly backed up to the ridge. A rented truck held tubs packed with ice and soda, as well as five-gallon water coolers. The fabricated Old West town was below the ridge, well out of camera range.

"Got the horses ready?" the second-unit director asked Rob.

She nodded. She liked the older woman, with her salt-and-pepper hair. There was an "equal to the task" way about her. "Boxed in the draw back there."

"All right. After the director shoots the close-up of Elise astride Death Threat, the horses are to be driven out."

"Colt will take care of that."

"Right," the woman said crisply. "You stand by for a long shot of you on Death Threat, leading the mares out of the canyon."

Rob nodded again. A red scarf bound her hair, and she missed her hat. She felt uncomfortable in the flounced red skirt and low white blouse, identical to what Elise was wearing. The blouse showed too much flesh, even though she had yanked it up higher on her chest. She felt almost naked, the way she had this morning, inside the barn.

Her gaze slid over to Jed Pulaski. He was talking softly, earnestly, to Elise, who was sitting in a high-legged chair with her name stenciled across its canvas back. A parasol had been anchored to it to protect her delicate skin from the blistering sun. Jed's big hands were planted on both chair arms, and his expression was serious, concentrated. Every so often, Elise nodded. Then, as if satisfied, Jed patted her shoulder and helped her down out of the chair.

He beckoned to Marcie, the makeup artist, who hurried over with her caddie. Quickly, efficiently, the girl dabbed the perspiration from Elise's forehead and repowdered her shiny face. Meanwhile, Jed went over the scene with the script supervisor. Linda was an intelligent-looking and very pretty young woman, Rob decided grudgingly, though for the life of her she couldn't figure out why a woman would paint blond streaks through brown hair. As crazy as spray-painting the horses.

Then there was Jack, with his hair painted almost white. He was complaining that the voices weren't being picked up on the remote mike. Someone else was shouting, "Is anyone from Wardrobe here?"

At last Jed called, "Quiet! We're rolling."

"Get it quiet, please!" the script supervisor echoed.

The second assistant cameraman held up the clapper that would help them synchronize the soundtrack with the film later.

"Action!" Jed said.

Elise moved into camera range, striding toward Death Threat. Doyle Reese stood just out of sight, holding a rope that had been spray-painted black so it would be hidden against the stallion's coat.

"All right," Jed coached from behind the camera. "Right here, honey. Look right here."

The wild abandon Elise's features were supposed to express was muted by the wariness that seeped into her eyes as she approached the horse.

"Go tight on that," Jed instructed the cameraman.

Grasping Death Threat's mane, Elise struggled to pull herself onto his back. Her motions weren't the smooth, accomplished actions of a young woman who had grown up in a Gypsy camp. Equally unexpected was Death Threat's sudden sidestepping. With a shriek, Elise slid off and rapidly scrambled on all fours away from his dancing hooves.

"Cut!" Jed yelled.

Doyle Reese had yanked savagely on the rope and was lashing the rearing animal with his whip. "Whoa, you bastard!"

Self-defense was one thing, but needless brutality was another. Rob started to intervene, but just as quickly checked herself. The horse belonged to Reese.

Instead she shouldered her way through the press of gaping people surrounding the shaken Elise. Heavy mascara streaked one cheek and mingled with the dust on the girl's skin. Jed pushed past Rob to cup Elise's jaw and tilt it up for his inspection. "You all right, honey?"

"I think so," the girl said in an unsteady voice.

Rob rolled her eyes. If the actress couldn't handle a horse, any horse, then the picture was in real trouble.

"Ready to have another go at it?" he asked gently.

Elise turned teary eyes up at him. "Do we have to use such a big horse?"

He smiled reassuringly. "Yes, for perspective, so the audience knows how petite you are—as opposed to the hero's wife."

His reasoning seemed to appeal to her. She nodded slowly, her lips pressed together in valiant resignation. "I'll try."

"Good girl."

He turned back to Reese. "That's what we want this horse for—spirit. Forget the whip."

Doyle Reese's sullen expression faded somewhat at Jed's peremptory instructions. "Right."

Next Jed focused his criticism on Rob. "As the wrangler, you're paid to work with the animals. This shouldn't have happened. One of your jobs will be to advise Elise on how to carry out the scene with Death Threat. Understand?"

Rob managed a noncommittal nod. There were moments when she wondered if what she got paid was worth hassling with Jed Pulaski.

She turned to the girl. "Listen," she said in a patient voice, "that isn't a hack you've got to ride. Death Threat's got a good mind, and if you act like you don't, it's going to bother him. Don't sit on him like a lump. You aren't a sack of pinto beans. But don't go all stiff like a stone statue, either. Get my drift?"

Elise nodded, but her lips quivered.

Jed listened with a droll curve to his mouth. For once he seemed bemused, and Rob wondered if she had missed some of the finer points of her instructions. But no, she was certain she had spoken as plainly as she needed to in order to make a city girl understand.

He appeared to recollect himself and snapped his fingers, calling, "Makeup."

Marcie reappeared with her caddie, swathed her sponge over Elise's upturned face and applied Vaseline to her full, pouty lips.

The assistant cameraman held up the slate indicating take 2. Chin thrust out resolutely, Elise moved into camera range, grabbed Death Threat's mane and hauled herself astride his back to sit rigidly. Rob thought the girl looked like one of those storefront wooden Indians.

"All right, honey," Jed coaxed, "lean forward... that's it...whisper in his ear...now gently dig your heels into his flanks." He turned to Doyle. "Reese, you run along ahead until—"

At the touch of Elise's heels, Death Threat shot forward like a racehorse at the sound of the starting bell. The rope was jerked from Reese's hands. Screaming, Elise clung to the horse's mane as he streaked across the ridge. Death Threat plunged down into a gulch and a moment later galloped up the opposite bank—without Elise.

"Cut!" Jed shouted and took off running. Rob matched him stride for stride. They arrived at the crest of the gulch simultaneously and stared down at Elise, who lay crumpled at the bottom.

"God almighty," Jed breathed, and scrambled down the gravelly slope.

Rob half slid right behind in the dust he stirred up. By the time they reached the bottom, Elise was struggling to sit up. A deep crimson slash curved around her right cheekbone, and one arm jutted at an unnatural angle. She groaned. Then her eyes rolled back, and she fainted into Jed's arms.

He glanced up at Rob and snapped, "I thought you told her how to ride this animal?"

She started to explain that the horse's behavior wasn't natural. Instead, with a grunt of disgust, she spun away and left Jed with Elise. If she didn't find Death Threat first, Reese would whip the stallion within an inch of his life, and that wouldn't do anyone any good.

Chapter 6

Jed turned off his car's engine. A light was on in the ranch house, even though it was after one in the morning. He rested his forehead against the steering wheel for a moment, then rubbed the bridge of his nose. That morning's call had been an early one, five-thirty, and he was bushed. The long wait this evening through three hours of surgery hadn't helped. He was a man who went for the thrill and had no patience when it came to empty time slots in his life.

He got out of the Porsche, and the ranch dog, D.O.G., trotted over to greet him. The dog looked to be a cross between a shepherd and a coyote. "You still awake, my fine canine friend?" Scratching the dog's head, he glanced up at the single lighted window. "Along with your master, eh?"

With weary steps, he entered the big house and made his way through the darkness toward the staircase. He figured that if he could drop off immediately, which he rarely did, he would wind up with three hours' sleep. He frequently got by on a lot less—like none—usually when he was writing on location. Following one of those marathon writing periods he would hang a Do Not Disturb sign on his hotel door and sleep around the clock.

"Mr. Pulaski?"

Taken by surprise, Jed halted at the first stair and glanced across the balustrade. What he saw might have been one of those hallucinations that came with an excess of liquor. Except that he didn't drink that much at one time anymore—and the vision was a very real young woman with the unraveled mass of her hair cascading sleekly over her shoulders. His gaze traveled from her white cotton robe's high neckline down past her white pajama bottoms to settle on bare toes free of nail polish.

"No, you're no pink elephant," he murmured.

A puzzled frown drew those marvelous thick brows together. Then she asked, "Is she all right? Elise?"

He nodded and ran his hand through his rumpled hair. "Yeah, if you count a broken arm and thirteen stitches in your cheek as all right. What are you doing still up?"

"Oh, er...reading." She waved vaguely toward her brother's office.

She didn't look like the type to seclude herself with a book. "Your brother have anything to drink in his office?"

Her expression scoffed at his question. "We have milk or coffee."

Caffeine wasn't going to make sleeping any easier, and he hadn't drunk milk in years. Surely that old Indian had a cache of booze somewhere.

"Fresh milk," she added. "From Miss Behaviour."

Fresh milk. His grunt was a statement of a city-raised boy's revulsion. "Your family," he said dryly, "has an imaginative system for naming its animals. Well, I suppose I can manage to down a glass."

He started to follow her as she padded silently down the darkened hallway to the kitchen, but the glimpse of the comfortable leather couch in the office teased his bone-tired body. "I'll take that glass in the office," he said, and headed straight for the couch.

He nudged aside a book that lay facedown on one cushion, but curiosity prompted him to pick it up. Stretching out, he peeked at the title. *A College Treasury of World Literature.* Definitely not the sort of thing he would have expected Rob to be reading. He turned to where she had left off. A wry smile tugged at the corners of his mouth.

She entered the room, and he glanced up from *The Importance of Being Earnest.* "Exploring Oscar Wilde, are you?" he drawled.

With her skin so tanned, it should have been impossible for her to blush, but he would have sworn she did just that. "My brother's college textbook." She shoved the glass of milk at him. "There."

Amused, he watched as she plopped into the wide leather chair across from the couch and folded her arms. Her fiery eyes stared him down. "I just wanted to know what was so all-fired important about the guy."

He nodded, this time careful to keep the laughter from his voice. He thought he might tell her how Wilde had spent time in prison for being "different." After all, Rob had a sister-in-law who had also undergone the unforgettable experience of being in prison, and she might just find the story of interest. But instead he talked about what was foremost in his mind. "Elise's injuries put her out of the picture."

He sat up and downed the milk in one gulp. Not bad. Not bad at all. He set the empty glass on a rustic end table and, clasping his hands between his spread knees, focused all his attention on the defiant young woman opposite him. "I want you to take over the role of the Gypsy girl."

"What?"

He had astonished himself, as well. Until this moment he hadn't given the idea a flicker of a thought. But, yes, staring at her now, with her dark hair loose and abandoned and framing her willful face...it might just work. "You're ten years older than the part calls

for, but you don't look it. And your features have a
Gypsy cast to them. A wild, passionate Gypsy."

His eyes narrowed as he surveyed her critically.
Ironically, what he had been looking for Elise to imi-
tate, this young woman actually had—a sort of ripe
adolescent longing. Her face was right out of a Botti-
celli painting. She was utterly different from anybody
else. There was an otherworldly quality about her. But
could she act?

Under his scrutiny, she stiffened, sitting almost re-
gally in her chair. "No. I won't do it. So don't look at
me that way, Mr. Pulaski."

That was rich! "Not even for one hundred and
twenty thousand dollars?"

Her long lashes flickered at the sum, which must
have been staggering to her. She paused, biting her
lower lip. She was fighting the lure he had tossed her
and succeeding—though not without some difficulty,
he noted.

"Not even for that," she finally said.

The stubborn set of her enchanting mouth told him
that he was wasting his time. But if he'd learned one
thing in Hollywood, it was that everyone had a price.
He relaxed, lacing his fingers behind his head and
stretching out his legs so that his tennis shoes were
wedged on either side of her bare feet. Her toes curled
under, as if demonstrating her out-of-character bash-
fulness.

"I thought you wanted that cutting-horse ranch?"
he said in a lazy drawl.

"I do, and one day I'll get it."

"When you're as old as Red Eye and can barely hobble around?"

Her gaze veered away from his. She bit her lip again. Her eyes returned to his, and he saw her dislike for him reflected there. "I can't!" It was a cry of pain.

"You can." He lowered his voice to a soft, compelling level. "I think there's nothing you haven't tried that you haven't succeeded at. And if anyone can ride the hell out of that devil, you can."

She shot up from her chair and began to pace in front of him. "Maybe, but I haven't ever tried acting. And I can't do it!" She wasn't looking at him, but stared blindly at the handwoven rag rug.

He rose and crossed to her, grasping her shoulders. They weren't soft and sloping like most women's, but supple and solidly set. "Then how do you know you can't do it until you try it?"

"I just know!" she cried. Private anguish smoked the pure green depths of her eyes. "It would be like I was naked. All those strangers looking inside me!"

She was original. Full of strange contrasts and with a sagacious grace. Yes, she would be perfect. He pulled her against him and stroked her hair. The strands clung to his hand. It was the desert's dry, static-filled air, he told himself, but his writer's imagination half believed that her hair was as willful as she was. He tilted her chin, forcing her to meet his eyes, and his voice took on a husky quality. "I want you to trust me, Rob. I won't demand anything of you that you're unwilling to give. I'll be there—between you and the outside world. I promise."

Rob frowned into the mirror. She didn't like all that gooey makeup on her face. It made her feel as if her skin were smothering. And her hair—she didn't like it all tousled and curled like bedsprings. She fidgeted beneath the plastic cape.

"Hold still," Marcie chided her. Impatiently she pushed her blond ponytail out of the way and bent over Rob again. "You'll make me smear the lip liner."

Rob drew in a fortifying breath. The makeup room in the compact trailer allowed very little movement, what with the long counter running the trailer's length and the other chairs in front of it. She ached to stretch her long legs. "I look like I was made up by Sherwin-Williams," she mumbled.

Marcie grunted in exasperation. "There! I've gone and smeared the pencil."

"I thought that people in the Old West didn't wear makeup," Rob grumbled.

"Listen, try not to talk until I'm finished, all right?" She hovered over Rob again. "They didn't wear makeup. At least, most of them didn't. All I'm doing is just defining your lips so the lights won't wash your color away. Your mouth is striking, you know."

It wasn't a question. The pretty blonde was just making conversation. More talking, Rob thought wearily.

"A makeup artist needs to capitalize on an actor's assets. Like your mouth, for instance."

Marcie stepped back and peered speculatively at Rob. "Your eyebrows—we need to do something with them. Too thick." She picked up a small brush and stroked the ends of Rob's brows with an experimental touch. "No go," she sighed. "We're going to have to pluck them."

Rob pulled off the cape and stood up. "No, you're not. I like them just the way they are."

"I didn't mean it like that. It's just that they're way too thick. If you'd just let me do something toward the ends, your face would—"

Rob didn't wait to hear the rest. She dropped the cape in the swivel chair and stalked from the trailer. She found Jed on the saloon set, conversing with Tor. Pushing past the greensman, who was toting a large potted fern, she confronted Jed with her fists on her hips. "I won't do it."

"Won't do what?"

"I won't let that girl pluck my eyebrows!"

He glanced past her, and she turned to see the makeup artist hurrying toward them. "Mr. Pulaski," she said breathlessly, "I was just trying to explain to her how much crisper her features would look."

Jed cupped Rob's chin and angled it one way and then another. "Hmmm."

"I won't do it!" She tried to jerk her chin from his grasp, but he held it fast.

"Her instincts are right, Marcie. I think plucking would make her appear too civilized."

"Of course, Mr. Pulaski," the makeup artist said and backed away.

"And another thing," Rob said.

Jed exhaled impatiently. "I knew that just one complaint was too much to hope for, Malcolm."

"It's my hair." She tugged on a springy coil. "I look like I got zapped by lightning."

His mouth stretched thin. "Your hair stays as it is—pagan."

Tor chuckled and drew Rob close. "Uncivilized . . . pagan. You make Rob sound like a cavewoman, Jed. She's the only one among us who isn't plastic."

Jed leveled his golden-brown eyes on her. He stared at her thoughtfully. It made her nervous. When others looked at her, they saw only a weathered young ranch woman. But he seemed to see inside her, to find something even she wasn't aware of. She couldn't imagine what it was, but it certainly gave him the advantage over her.

"You're right, Tor. That's why I didn't want her eyebrows plucked."

She stepped out of Tor's protective clasp. "Stop talking about me as if I'm not here."

"You're not going to be," Jed said. "You need to hoof it over to Wardrobe. We shoot in half an hour."

Wardrobe wasn't any better than Makeup. In the stifling semi, two women worked on her. She felt like a mannequin, standing stiffly as one wardrobe woman, on her knees, let out the hem of a bright turquoise tiered skirt. The other stood behind Rob, taking in a blouse that had been made for Elise to make it conform to Rob's smaller chest measurements. Both women wore carpenter's aprons, the pockets stuffed with tapes and safety pins and even a stapler.

Rob shook her head dourly. "This isn't me."

"Not supposed to be," one of the women mumbled, her lips clamped on half a dozen straight pins.

"You're supposed to be an exotic Mexican Gypsy," the other said. "You don't have enough bosom showing."

Rob's mouth tightened. "I don't have a bosom."

"Of course you do. It just needs to be emphasized." The wardrobe woman turned away to rummage in a box. "If I can only find that uplift bra..."

"What the hell do you think you're doing?" Landis screeched from the doorway.

"I beg your pardon, Miss Falkenberg?" the wardrobe woman on her knees mumbled. The pins in her mouth tumbled out onto the floor.

The other woman, searching for the bra, said quickly, "Is there something we can find for you?"

"You bet your buns." She held up a brown woolen dress. "You're providing little bitty costumes for anorexic teenagers! Get over to my dressing room with a costume that fits! Now!" She turned, but then her gaze fell on Rob. "I understand we're doing a scene together today."

Rob nodded.

"Don't try to steal it, honey," she said, "because I know more about upstaging than you could ever learn in a lifetime. Cross me, and in two days I'll have you back shoveling manure out of that barn of yours. Understand?"

She didn't even wait for Rob to answer before she swept out of the trailer. What had Marianna said about actors being temperamental? Obviously they were, and Rob supposed she herself was becoming one of them quickly, because she wasn't about to wear a contraption that shoved her breasts out in such a humiliating way.

This time she found Jed talking with Peter Maxwell on the boardwalk. The facade protected them from the biting sand whirled by the blustery afternoon wind. Jed looked up from his call sheet. "Yes?"

"Can I talk to you?"

"Okay, talk."

She glanced at the producer. A silver-haired fox, she thought. Her gaze slid back to Jed. "Alone. It's ... private."

Maxwell's brows, pure white and perfectly arched, lowered over eyes that evaluated her. Cash-register eyes. They switched over to Jed. "I'll talk to you later about this decision, Pulaski," he said in an icy tone.

Jed's eyes narrowed to slits. "You worry about the pennies, Maxwell. I'll worry about acting ability."

After Maxwell left, Jed thrust his hands into his jeans pockets. He wore a black T-shirt that was damp with sweat and clung to his broad chest and the flat plane of his stomach. She could have counted the muscled ridges there. Impatience was written all over his rugged features. "Well?"

She pushed away the hair that the wind whipped into her face, glanced around, then slipped into the slight corner created by two adjoining buildings. She nodded toward her bosom and whispered, "Look!"

He canted his head. "At what?"

She nodded again. "There."

His gaze raked down her throat to where her hands were crossed protectively at her chest. "If you'd move your hands," he said dryly, "I could tell what you're talking about."

"They're naked, you jackass!"

He rubbed the bridge of his nose, and she had the distinct impression that he was avoiding letting her see his expression. "Ah, yes, your breasts," he said, his words seeming smothered to her.

She tugged at the ruffled blouse. "It's too low."

When he finally looked at her, his expression was strained. "You wore one like it before."

"It didn't show all . . . this. I can't wear it. It's low enough for a whole herd to stampede through!"

He moved in closer, blocking off the wind that whistled past the jutting wall. His voice deepened, taking on an intimate quality. "You once told me, sweetheart, that 'teats is teats.' If a cow isn't bothered by her teats showing, why are you?" His finger trailed along her flesh, just above the ruffle line. Her skin felt seared. A burning sensation flowed through her like electricity, all the way down to her stomach. Branding couldn't be much more painful, she thought, trying to find her breath.

"Besides," he said softly, "the most beautiful parts of your breasts are still concealed, like hard, dusky pearls, waiting to be found."

She noticed that his eyes had a smoky cast to them, like the sky on an Indian summer day. By giving in to him, she felt as if she were losing a piece of herself, but she couldn't think of anything to back up her argument. Everything he'd said had sounded right. But she suspected he was playing with her again.

"I hate acting," she blurted. "Keep this up and there won't be any of me left."

With his knuckles, he brushed back the strands of hair clinging to her cheek. "Little by little, we all surrender parts of our freedom, of ourselves—and we're all hostages to something. I'm a hostage to my art. You're a hostage to your dream."

Landis watched from behind her dressing room's screen door as the young ranch woman stalked past Jed, watched as Jed's eyes followed the girl.

Quietly, thoughtfully, Landis crossed to the small refrigerator to pull out a tray of ice. Her hand was shaking as she dropped the cubes into a glass. "Damn," she muttered.

She poured a hefty shot of vodka and swirled it in the glass. Her gaze deserted the crystalline liquid and edged toward the mirror. With revulsion, she turned her back to it. It's beating me, she thought. Time is winning.

No, an inner voice protested. I'm still as good as I ever was.

A year or two, at most, and I'll look like a hag.

I already do in the morning, she thought dismally, and took another swallow of the vodka. It was powerful enough to curl her tongue like a window blind, stinging all the way down, burning clean a throat coated with too much nicotine.

This was her last chance, and if she didn't make it...then what? All the money she'd made over the years had gone to lovers, husbands, gigolos. The few investments she had made had been unwise. She had loved acting with every ounce of strength in her. She had no regrets that she had chosen this profession over being a housewife. Her life had been exciting, challenging and productive.

But now, if she didn't have another hit soon, all she had to look forward to was the Actors' Home for the Aged. She thought of the young ranch woman. Rob Malcolm had a presence that made you want to look at her. What if the camera picked up on that?

Landis turned and hurled her glass at the mirror. The sound of shattering glass drowned out her moan of fear.

"You've got to be out of your ever-loving mind, Pulaski!" Maxwell shouted.

Jed slumped in his chair, grateful for the shade of the boardwalk's awning, and ignored the other man's tirade. From inside the saloon came a terse exchange of opinions between the production designer and the art director. Nearby, Charley was rigging a special-effects prop. At the far end of the street, the crew had lined up at the catering wagon for juice and cold drinks. "Trust me, Maxwell," he said when the older man stopped to take a breath.

Hadn't he said the same to Rob Malcolm?

The producer loosened the knot of his blue silk tie. "Look," he said in his satin-lined voice, "if we don't bring this picture in under budget, the backers are going to balk like army mules."

They weren't the only ones who were going to balk, Jed thought grimly. It was obvious that Rob Malcolm was going to balk at every scene that demanded anything more of her than riding.

Beneath the blaze of the June sun, the producer was getting hot under the collar. Jed only tolerated the pompous Maxwell for the sake of the man's financial connections. Now Maxwell leaned forward in his chair and demanded, "Would you mind telling me just how on God's green earth you propose to make a movie audience buy a Mexican Gypsy with a Texas twang?"

"Professor Higgins did it," Jed answered laconically.

"Did what?"

"In Shaw's *Pygmalion*. If by changing the speech of a cockney girl a professor of phonetics could deceive the British aristocracy into believing the gutter-snipe was one of them, then I sure as hell can do it with Rob Malcolm. It's just a matter of getting the vowels right."

Maxwell's polished voice was silvered with derision. "You're going to play Pygmalion to her Galatea?" He almost snorted. "She'll fight you all the way!"

Jed smiled thinly. "No, I'm going to play Petruchio to Kate. I'm going to tame the shrew, Maxwell."

Chapter 7

The Border Bluff Trading Post was the local pool hall, bar, post office, feed store, dance hall and convenience store, since it was the only place within thirty miles of anything. A lone survivor of the frontier days, the flat-roofed adobe building straddled a low ridge overlooking the dry wash of Castalon Creek and the Mexican border. Its walls retained the scars of the raids of Pancho Villa.

For Rob, it was more than just a historic marker in a relentless, savage land. The memories the pock-marked trading post held were the markers of her life. It had been a rural hangout for generations of ranching and farming families in that part of Texas, New Mexico and old Mexico. Here her father had bought her first pair of chaps. Here she had tried Mexican beer and promptly thrown up. And here leathery old Emmitt had taught her to play pool, badgering her until the day finally came that she beat him. His usual grumpy expression had changed to one of pure pride on that occasion.

Here, too, she had observed the intricacies of courtship, had watched old and young alike seek dance partners at Saturday night's festive *bailes*. And sometimes they had sought much more. A partnership for life, she supposed. The idea made her feel suffocated. One person…always in your life, in your way…always talking, demanding a piece of you.

But then, she thought uneasily, what was it that Jed Pulaski had said about wolves? That they mated for life and grieved when their mates died? She had been right in comparing him to a wild dog rather than a wolf. He would never settle for just one mate. There was that "female entertainment lawyer keeping his California bed warm." That was what she'd overheard one of the wardrobe mistresses saying.

From what Rob could tell, Jed didn't spend that much time in bed. His bedroom was directly above hers, and she heard him pacing the floor most nights. Not her. The hard work and fresh air put her right to sleep. At least they used to—before he came.

Beneath her thick eyelashes, her gaze slid surreptitiously toward the man. Along with several members of the crew, he was lounging against a pickup parked near the trading post's patio. He had so much vitality, she thought, that he made the others look like zombies.

Linda was talking to him. Compared to Rob, the script supervisor was more his type, more his style. Sophisticated. Knowing. Rob watched Jed light Linda's cigarette. The two seemed to be laughing and joking and only half watching the merrymakers, who, dressed in their Saturday best, danced enthusiastically to everything from the Cotton-Eyed Joe to the schottische.

The dance floor was more crowded than usual because of the extras, cast and crew who had descended on the trading post in search of amusement.

Rob knew that she herself was one source of amusement for them. The locals knew better than to ask her to dance, but apparently one of the special-effects people hadn't heard that asking her was a waste of energy.

Charley, whose hair and skin had been turned golden by the California sun, swaggered over to stand before her, thumbs thrust inside the waistband of jeans tight enough to have been grafted to his skin. He nodded toward the band, a guitarist, a violinist and a trumpet player. "What would you say to a turn around the floor, babe?"

The light from lanterns suspended from the trading post's corrugated roof invaded the darkness beyond, where buckboards were parked alongside automobiles—and where certain males were watching expectantly. She could just imagine their arrogant grins.

With her boots on, she was over six feet. Now she slipped down from the cedar railing where she had been perched and stretched herself to her full height. "I don't think a puppy dog can handle a giant economy-size cat."

Charlie was tall enough—about six feet, too—but her formidable expression and contemptuous tone took some of the bite out of his swaggering cockiness. His grin turned more personal. "Why don't you give me the chance to prove I can?"

"You'd only prove yourself a fool," she drawled, and shouldered past him, heading inside toward the pool table. On Saturday nights it was taken off the wide covered patio and wedged in the back of the trading post along with the used saddles the cowboys left to be traded.

At the counter, she paused long enough to pay for a long-necked beer, then made her way toward the two cowboys swapping tall stories by the cooler.

"... cattle get sour and won't honor a horse."

"Hey, Emmitt," she called to Mescalero's grizzled ranch hand. "How about shooting a game of pool with me?"

Emmitt shifted the plug of chewing tobacco inside his lower lip, did his 85-mph blink and said, "Taught you too well. Can't run the table on you anymore."

"I can."

She knew that voice by now. With exaggerated slowness, she glanced over her shoulder. Jed was leaning against the counter. He was wearing khaki trousers and a tan shirt with the sleeves rolled to the elbows.

He paid for a can of beer and ambled down the aisle toward her. "Want to take me on, Malcolm?"

The man needed to be taken down a notch, she thought. "Eight-Ball or Cowboy?"

"You name it." He grinned cheerfully and followed her over to the table.

"I'll give you a fighting chance," she said, racking the balls. She was on her own turf now, and confident. "Eight-Ball."

His eyes measuring her, he balanced his beer can on the cue rack. "What are the stakes?" he asked, taking down a cue and chalking it.

She shrugged. There wasn't a ranch hand this side of the I-10 who could beat her. "Winner buys the next round of beer?"

He inclined his head and eyed her speculatively. "How about something more interesting?"

She heard the baiting tone in his voice. Her eyes narrowed. "Like what?"

"Say, your total cooperation. In making the film, for instance."

Her mouth narrowed in disgust. "I'm wearing that show-everything blouse, aren't I?"

"And angling away from the camera at every close-up." He fixed her with that compelling gaze of his. "If I win, you do exactly as I say. Agreed?"

"And if I win?" She held back her smirk. It had clearly never occurred to him that a woman might win.

"The choice is yours."

"There's nothing you have that I want."

"Are you certain?" His smile was challenging. "What about my teaching you to play polo?"

"Polo?"

"You know, horse hockey. Mounted mayhem."

"I know what polo is. I just didn't think you knew anything about riding."

"There's a lot I know that you aren't aware of."

She was thinking rapidly. Although she had on occasion trained cutting horses that ended up being used for polo, she had never thought about actually learning the game. Polo—the rich folk's game. She could learn to beat them in their own backyards. Yes, she would like that. Very much. "All right," she said with a negligent shrug. "It's a deal."

He leveled a steady gaze on her. "I give you fair warning, Malcolm. You're not playing with a tenderfoot."

"Neither are you, Pulaski."

"Would you like to break?"

She smiled thinly. Gallants and gents. You take your little shot, they think. Then I'll show you how to shoot pool.

She banked her opening shot, sending the orange five ball spinning into a pocket. "I'll pocket the three next," she told him without looking up. Bending over the table to get the right angle, she did just that.

She flicked him a triumphant look—only to find that he was observing not her skillful shot but her jean-clad backside. He switched his gaze to her face and smiled charmingly. "Very nice."

Rattled, she scratched on the following stroke.

He took over. "The nine in the side." The ball rolled neatly into the side pocket. "I'll take the six next." He walked around the table, leaned over and fired another shot, and the six ball dropped right in.

To cover her dismay, she took a swig of her beer, which was rapidly warming in her grip. "All right," she said, her tone grudging. "So you're good."

He grinned amiably. "I'm more than that. I'm great." He straightened and leaned on his cue. "Malcolm, I could string you along, but I like you, so I'm going to end your agony quickly."

She set her bottle down and tried on one of Marianna's sweet smiles. "A Polish joke, Pulaski?"

His eyes twinkled. "Merely the unvarnished truth." He hunched over the table again and called, "The four in the right pocket and the seven in the left."

Uneasily she observed the way he played the stick almost sensually back and forth between his fingers, gaining familiarity with its weight and balance. Then he knocked the cue ball into the remaining cluster of balls. The four ball jumped the others and hurtled toward the right pocket. In amazement, she watched the seven ball ricochet off the far cushion and spin into the left pocket. Her stomach churned with alarm.

As he ran the rest of the table, he talked in pleasant, conversational tones. "You see, Malcolm, I used to shoot pool with the sharks. If you were part of

Pittsburgh's street scene, you learned two things—how to protect yourself and how to shoot pool. Let that be a lesson to you. Know everything there is to know about your opponent before you take him on. And never underestimate him.''

He paused, called the eight ball's pocket, then sent the black ball rolling. "Not bad," he said, straightening to watch it plunk into the designated pocket. "Although in my younger days, when I played pool all the time, I could finish off a game in four shots."

Dazzled, she watched him slide the cue back into its slot. He turned back to her. "Shall we dance?"

"I feel like a fool," she muttered, still dazed by his performance.

He took her arm and steered her toward the screen door. "Don't. There's always somebody better out there."

Only when he took her into his arms did she realize that he intended to walk her onto the dance floor. She pushed at his shoulders. "I don't dance."

He pulled her back into his embrace. "You do now."

"I will not—"

His arm tightened around her waist. "Uh-uh. Remember our wager. You do exactly as I say."

Her eyes flared. "We were talking about me acting in your film."

"As I recall, we didn't limit it to that." His eyes took on a reproachful cast. "I didn't figure you to be the kind to welsh on a bet, Malcolm."

Her direct gaze entreated him, and her voice sounded cracked to her own ears. "Do I have to do this?"

His mouth twitched in a dry grin. "Think of it as part of your development as an actress."

She squinched her eyes up and moaned. "Damn it, I can't dance! I *can't*!"

He grinned with an infuriating certainty. "You will, Annie Oakley, because you have too much Malcolm pride to back down now. Not with everyone watching."

She didn't know much about Annie Oakley, but she knew for sure that he was right about everyone watching. Beneath the country-and-western strains of the music, she could hear the hum of astonishment circulating through the trading post.

Rob Malcolm dancing! Imagine that! Next thing you know, it'll be snowing in July.

A fiery heat traveled from her feet all the way up to tingle her scalp. She would have given anything to be wearing her slouch hat to hide her face. But she wasn't, so she squared her shoulders, hitched up her jeans and put her arm on his shoulder and her hand in his.

He put his hand on the back of her head and nudged it against his cheek. "Not so stiff," he whispered into her ear.

His warm breath made her tingle again, in a different way this time. She tried to draw away slightly, but he held her firmly. She could feel his entire body, from his thighs against hers to his chest, hard, yet compelling.

Beyond, she could see Tom pushing Marianna across the sand-sprinkled floor in his best Texas Two-Step. At the sight of her in Jed's arms, her brother did a double take. So did Bronco Bobby, who was whirling his wife Ruthie around the floor. Bobby's amazed grin showed that he still hadn't fixed his teeth. If he had, the entire territory would have known the next day. Just as, by tomorrow morning, the news of her dancing with Jed would be breakfast talk over every ranch-house table.

Rob was chagrined, and the next thing she knew she stepped on Jed's foot with her heavy boot. He muttered a curse.

"Oh, I'm sorry!" Lord, this was awful, everyone watching her plod across the dance floor like a heifer heavy with calf! If only she could evaporate. "I told you," she grated. "I told you I couldn't dance!"

If she had hoped to flee the dance floor, she was destined for disappointment, because he didn't let her. His hand pressed against her spine, arching her into him. "Listen, Rob, take the advice you gave to Elise the day she tried to ride Death Threat. Remember? Don't go all stiff as a statue on me, but don't go limp as a sack of pinto beans, either. All right?"

Realizing that she was doomed to finish out the dance, she could only nod. She closed her eyes so she wouldn't have to see the watching faces. How had her life become so disrupted? Her private feelings exposed to everyone . . . her private thoughts invaded by this man. He wasn't even a cowboy, for heaven's sake. But he *had* said he could ride. If he could ride the way he shot pool, then he could ride like a Comanchero.

"This isn't so bad, is it?"

Her eyes snapped open. "What?"

"Dancing." His warm breath tickled her ear, and all sorts of strange sensations zephyred through her.

"Dancing?" she repeated in a bemused voice.

She heard him chuckle. "Yeah, Malcolm. What we're doing right now."

Her gaze darted over the dance floor. Why, they had circled it entirely without her making another misstep. When she had relaxed and yielded to Jed, letting him lead her, her awkwardness had disappeared. She tilted her head back, a somewhat abashed grin curving her mouth. "There's nothing to it, is there?"

"Like I told you, nothing to—" He groaned as her boot caught his instep this time. "Come on," he said.

He tugged her off the dance floor, past the crowd of onlookers, past Red Eye, who was doing some kind of private war dance, his moccasined feet beating a primitive rhythm against the sand, most likely because Tom had confiscated his cache of sotol.

Beyond the trading post, cars and pickups were parked. Some had their headlights shining for couples who could find no room to dance under the covered porch. Jed weaved his way between the parked vehicles. "I think some private lessons are in order, Malcolm."

She yanked her hand from his. "No."

They were standing between a flatbed wagon and a pickup. The brilliant disk of the moon gilded his face, throwing it into relief, highlights contrasting with shadows. She imagined that his hair was the color of the Spanish gold Coronado and his conquistadores had searched for. And his eyes had darkened to deep brown. "Malcolm," he growled softly, "I'm not accustomed to being thwarted, and I'm getting awfully tired of reminding you of your bargain."

He held out his hand again, waiting.

With great reluctance, she laid her hand in his open palm. "I don't want to dance anymore," she whispered in an anguished voice.

"Why not? There's no one here to see if you make a mistake."

It was being alone with a man...this man...held in his arms.

His gaze met hers. "What is it?" he asked.

"You." Why didn't she have the tongue of a politician in a reelection year? Why couldn't she speak cleverly enough to preserve her dignity?

His hand closed over hers, and she could feel the heat flowing from him, seeping through his veins, weakening the independence she was so proud of. "What about me?" he asked.

She glanced away. Plain talking was so difficult. "I feel all funny...unsure...around you."

"That's not what I want." Slowly he drew her toward him. "I want you to feel very sure about yourself when you're with me."

She stared at his mouth. She liked it. It was strong, firm. She especially liked the way his scar lifted his lip slightly. She eyed him suspiciously. "You aren't going to kiss me again, are you?"

His hands settled on either side of her waist, anchoring her narrow hips against his. "Is that what you want?"

She tilted her head to one side, considering. "No, I don't think so."

Laughter rumbled in his throat, and she tried to pull away. "No, don't," he said. "I'm not laughing at you. I'm laughing at me. In my egocentricity, I pompously assume that all women are interested in me—if not for myself, then for the pleasure I can give them." He caught her chin, making her look at him. "For whatever reason, though, most women enjoy being kissed."

She nodded. "I figured that. Just can't figure out why."

She could tell he was trying not to laugh again when he asked, "You didn't enjoy our kiss?"

She thought again. "Well, yes. And no."

This time he smiled. His hands still at her hips, he backed up a step to lean against a pickup fender, drawing her with him. "Why yes? And why no?"

She shook her head. "I don't know, exactly. It's like acting, I suppose. You take pieces of me. No, that's not quite it. Because after you kissed me, I felt too full of myself...like there was more of me. Oh, I don't know."

"Well, then, why don't we try that kiss one more time and find out?"

She searched his face, trying to determine whether he was toying with her again, the way Phrank toyed with a mouse. No, Jed's amber eyes were crystal-clear, his gaze steady, his mouth solemn. "All right."

His lips curved in a half smile. "You have to close your eyes, you know. That way you won't be distracted and can concentrate entirely on the kiss."

Obediently she closed her eyes. He was wrong, she realized. You noticed things *more* without your sight. The music from the trading post seemed distant, drifting. Yet its insistent beat was echoed by her pulse. The night air was cool and smelled of vegetation and dew. Then she felt his fingertip grazing her bottom lip.

"You should relax, Rob. Like you do when you're riding, or dancing. Don't hold your mouth so tightly."

She tried to do as he said, and his finger gently nudged her lips apart. "Sensuous," he murmured. Then she felt the pressure of his mouth on hers, moving lightly, softly. She got the feeling that he was experimenting with the kiss, seeking the right sensation. She did the same, moving her lips ever so gently with his, tasting him. Without really meaning to, she let her body relax into his, and her hands began to caress the hard wall of his chest.

"Mmmm," she breathed, and was surprised to hear the sound coming from her.

"Makes you want more, doesn't it?" he asked, his breath playing over her moistened lips.

She didn't want to open her eyes. "Yes ... yes, it does. Please, kiss me again."

For a moment she thought he hadn't heard her. She peered at him through the dense sweep of her lashes. He was frowning at her. Startled, she started to pull away, but his hands closed on either side of her face, holding her immobile. "No," he said.

Then he bent his head over hers and did as she had asked. She sighed at the silky friction of his mouth and nestled against him. When his tongue penetrated between her lips, she stiffened, feeling the surging, scalding heat, just as she had when he had kissed her in the prop trailer. Not just her lips, but all of her, seemed to go moist and damp. Every part of her felt oversensitized, afire. It was as if she had been racing against the wind, so that there wasn't an atom of air left in her lungs.

He shifted his weight into her, and she felt the hard ridge beneath his jeans, pressing against her belly, seeking. Her lids flew open. He raised his head, and his prowling eyes studied her face for a moment. A blistering heat flushed her skin.

"I think," he said quietly, "that you'd be very, very wise not to ask just any man to kiss you, Malcolm. Most of all me."

Shyloh hugged the shadows created by the trading post's L-shaped wall—and hugged her pain within her as she watched the dancing couples. Joy and love were imprinted on some faces—like those of Bobby and his wife, Ruthie. Others had impassioned faces, like the young makeup artist, Marcie, for one. And why shouldn't her eyes be shining, her lips parted expectantly? She was talking to Colt. He was lounging against his pickup, one boot propped on the front bumper, and Marcie was standing near him. Near enough for him to take her in his arms if he wanted.

Trouble was, you couldn't tell by his expression whether he wanted to or not. You couldn't ever tell anything Colt was thinking if you went strictly by his expression. Or, for that matter, if you went by what he said, since he didn't say more than was necessary, and even then, he never touched on his emotions.

Shyloh could tell a lot, though, from Marcie's expression. The young woman was intrigued by Colt. Her head was tilted, her lips parted, her lashes at half-mast. Colt Kahze was different. It wasn't enough that he was a cowboy. He was half-Indian, too. And that made him seem more dangerous, and all the more appealing.

But Marcie didn't know Colt the way Shyloh did. Marcie saw no farther than the brooding black eyes; she couldn't see the gentleness toward all creatures that was buried deep in his heart. It was amazing that that gentleness should exist when he was shunned by the other ranching families. Oh, not over coffee, or riding the pastures, or at roundup. But here, at the trading post, when socializing often led to the consolidation of families in marriage, Colt was an outcast. Tom Malcolm's bastard.

The Anglo families might have political power, the Hispanics might have aristocratic blood, but an Indian ... an Indian had nothing.

That was why, if Marcie was angling for a dance with Colt, she was doomed to disappointment. Colt didn't dance. But at least he treated the makeup artist like a woman, which was better than being treated like a kid sister.

Hurting, Shyloh forced her gaze away from the couple and back to the dance floor. She saw Rand approaching Haydee, who was leaning against one of the building's cedar posts. Shyloh could tell that her older brother was asking Mescalero's chef for a dance. The young woman glanced away, then shook her head. No. Rand shrugged and made his way back to a group of cowboys, who were drinking and joking and grinning like idiots.

Well, Shyloh thought, I suppose I'm not the only one doomed to have a broken heart.

But that knowledge made it no easier when the band began playing a country-and-western version of "Born Too Late."

Chapter 8

Rob stood on the fringe of the set and watched the scene in which Tor attempted to make friends with the wild mustang, who rejected the homesteader. Tor didn't appear too pleased about doing the scene. "We can't use a stand-in horse?" he asked Jed.

Jed ran his fingers through his shaggy hair. "Look, Tor, the horse is the focus of the story. We have to go with the real thing."

"Well, thank God and the story line I don't have to ride the beast," Tor said.

But Rob *did* have to ride Death Threat. If time permitted this afternoon, she would be doing a touching scene in which the Gypsy girl realized that she would risk being shot by the furious ranchers by going to see the horse. She expected that she would have to battle

Death Threat tooth and nail in order to bring off what Jed wanted. That stallion had a mean streak clear through him. While she might admire his spirit, she was determined that she was going to master the horse, not the other way around.

"Miss Malcolm?" a voice demanded behind her.

She turned around and sighed; it was the speech coach Jed had hired for her. The stiff-necked old woman was as mulish as Death Threat. "Another speech lesson?"

Miss Hawthorn nodded crisply, pursed her lips and glanced at her practical wristwatch. "It's precisely 2:00 p.m., Miss Malcolm."

Rob thought that with that gray hair and colorless face you could have stood the woman up against a weathered clapboard building and lost sight of her. With an inner groan, she followed Miss Hawthorn back to the trailer that housed the cast's dressing rooms. Rob's name had been inserted in the slot on the door to hers. Careful to duck her head so as not to bang the low lintel, she stepped inside. Her room, like the others, wasn't much larger than a horse stall and held a cushioned bench across from a dressing table and mirror, and had a tiny bathroom.

Miss Hawthorn took her seat at one end of the bench, and Rob dutifully took the other end. "Now, then, Miss Malcolm," the old woman began, "we need to retrain your speech, to develop an underlying Latin intonation. It's all in listening with a fine ear. What you have to remember is to use more than just your tongue for pronunciation. You must speak precisely. Use your throat, your lips, your entire mouth. Am I making myself understood?''

"Precisely," Rob mimicked.

"No, no," the old woman said, missing Rob's jest. "You hold your lips like so when pronouncing the *P*." Using her fingers, she pushed in at either side of Rob's mouth. "Now try it."

Rob rolled her eyes and mumbled, "I can't, when you're poking at me that way."

"Now, now, dear. Calm down and speak clearly."

Rob pushed the old woman's hands away. "That's it. No more!"

The woman's thin brows climbed. "What is it?"

Rob shot up from the couch and yanked open the door, only to hit her head. "Damn trailer doors!" she muttered.

Jed must have guessed by her face when she stalked onto the set that she'd reached the end of her patience. "Cut!" he called.

It didn't matter that the extras and crew were all watching. She strode toward him, her expression matching his for fury. The scar in his lip was pure white against his tanned face, and it drew his lip up in a snarl.

"That speech woman has her tail in the air because I'm not talking like she wants me to," she told him tersely. "The Spanish I speak doesn't sound anything like what she's been teaching."

"That's because you speak Tex-Mex," Jed pointed out with an expression that clearly indicated the fact that his patience was strained to the snapping point.

Behind her, the old woman stormed past the cast and crew. "Mr. Pulaski! I have worked with actors from almost every race and nationality, but never have I had the ill fortune to try to teach a woman who insists on speaking as if she has marbles in her mouth!"

Jed glanced back at Rob.

"Well," she said, "I can't talk when that woman has her fingers jammed in my mouth like a curb bit."

His lips a single thin line, he raised his eyes to the ceiling for a count of five. Then, even though he spoke to Miss Hawthorn, his smoking gaze was fixed on Rob. "I can appreciate your dilemma, Miss Hawthorn. Allow me a few words alone with Miss Malcolm."

His hand around her upper arm, he towed her behind the dry goods store. The wind was fierce and hot and tangled her already wild hair. "Listen, Malcolm," he said in an exacting tone that reminded her of Miss Hawthorn, "it's either the speech coach or me. But you *will* learn to speak properly. You *do* remember our agreement? Now, which will it be?"

She thought a moment. She studied his face, the way the desert sun and dry air had etched new lines around his eyes and deepened the creases bracketing his mouth. She recalled Miss Hawthorn's wrinkled face so close to hers, and she thought about the woman's bony fingers clamped around her jaw. "I think I'd rather have you touching me."

He blinked, then frowned, glancing away to the black mesa that loomed behind the set. Finally he stared back at her, his eyes the color of sun-heated desert sand. "Why did you have to be such a damned innocent?" he asked in frustration.

Death Threat was handsome in a rangy way. He reminded Rob a little of Jed. In temperament, too. Uncontrollable. No, worse. Most times, the mustang acted purely crazy. She found it hard to believe that any horse could be so mean, so unpredictable. Indifferent one moment, killer-crazed the next.

But if Death Threat disliked humans in general, he hated Doyle Reese. Anytime the man came around, the horse started whinnying and stomping and pawing the earth. True, Reese was unnecessarily rough on the animal, but not that rough. Reese stood ready now, whip in one hand, rope in the other, as Rob approached for the next shot. The man didn't like her, either—he didn't like any of the Malcolms—so she didn't trust him to restrain Death Threat.

"Know your lines, Malcolm?" Jed asked from behind the camera.

She grimaced but nodded. Reading the script, reading in general, was punishment to her—unless the subject was horses.

"All right," Jed said. "Do you want a rehearsal, or do you want to go straight into the scene?"

She wanted to get it over with. She wanted the entire movie over with, so she could get on with her life. "Straight into it."

"All right," he muttered. "Quiet! Right here, sweetheart," he said, turning to Rob. "Look at me."

He stepped behind the camera, and she turned her full attention to becoming the young Gypsy woman.

"Everybody ready to roll?" Jed asked.

"Quiet, please!" called Linda.

"Roll camera," he said.

"Rolling!" the young woman yelled.

Rob began walking toward Death Threat. Today he seemed high-strung and even more nervous than she was—but the script called for him to behave that way. "*Dulcemente, dulcemente,* my wild, handsome one," she said, her voice coaxing as she drew near.

Death Threat kept tossing his head. His eyes were abnormally wide, his ears were laid back threateningly. Rob stroked his neck, and he snorted warningly, but the script called for her to mount him now, so she stepped closer. Then, winding her fingers in his thick mane, she easily hauled herself astride. "There, now, that wasn't so bad, was it? Even a king must yield to a Gypsy princess."

Death Threat didn't agree. He began twisting and rearing. She knew that the director in Jed would love that, but it was up to her to master the horse by the scene's end. And this hotheaded mustang wasn't responding to anything she tried. It would have helped if she'd had a bridle and saddle to work with, but since she didn't, she dug in her knees. He shook his head and danced. "Easy, there, fella."

That wasn't in the script, but she didn't hear Jed calling "Cut!" What did happen was worse. Someone started the engine of a pickup off camera. "Kill that truck!" yelled Linda.

As a practical joke, one of the crew shouted, "Bang! Bang!"

At that, Death Threat seemed to go berserk. He began bucking wildly now, his eyes rolling, foaming at the mouth. Rob clung to him with all her strength, but the stallion rolled sharply to the right, and she went sailing. A spindly ocotillo caught her in its prickly arms. Thorns pierced her flesh from her nape to her knees, but her pain was nothing compared to her fury. She shot up from the ground and stormed back toward the rearing horse, which Reese was trying to restrain.

"You ornery son of a bitch," she told the stallion. "I'm gonna ride you yet!"

"Cut!" Jed yelled.

Embarrassment at having been thrown colored her face with crimson, although her mishap—and the engine noise, for that matter—wouldn't have ruined the scene. Here and there she caught a smirk on the faces of the crew. Jed stalked toward her, his eyes smoking. He brushed aside the first-aid man who was hovering beside her.

"Damn it, Malcolm! You spoiled a perfect take. A Mexican Gypsy doesn't say 'you ornery son of a bitch'!"

An earlier scene flitted through Rob's mind—of Jed bending solicitously over Elise after the starlet had been thrown. I should have swooned! Rob thought.

Instead of swooning, she decided to belt the man. Square in his belly. He gasped and doubled over. The grips, the cameramen and sound technicians, the gaffers and the first-aid man—everyone went silent. Ignoring their astonishment, she strode past the gaping crew and stalked toward her dressing room.

Rob Malcolm had yet to answer to him for that right hook to his gut yesterday. In the blacker recesses of his mind, he could conjure up a dozen ways to extract vengeance—the most delightful being to subject her to forty-five takes of a heavily emotional scene. He knew that acting, for her, was an agony of unveiling her inner self, both to the strangers on the set and to the camera itself. The opportunity for revenge was on the agenda this afternoon. The revised call sheet indicated that the initial seduction scene was up for shooting at four.

He located Tor in the makeup trailer. Marcie was dabbing Vaseline on the man's lips. Tor winked lewdly at Jed. "What wouldn't a thousand red-blooded American males give to be in my place," he mumbled against the girl's greased fingertips.

"Hold still," she said, ignoring the hand that tweaked her bottom.

Jed genuinely liked Tor, but today the man made him edgy. "Unfortunately, Tor, the girl's wasted on you."

"Your problem, Jed, is that *you* waste women." Tor leaned toward the mirror and viewed his image from one angle and then another. With long, supple fingers, he curled a wave of black hair into place over his forehead.

"You're being bitchy, Tor."

Tor swung around in the swivel chair to face Jed. "No, I'm being frank. I'll go on being honest and admit that since women pursue you, the consequences are their own problem. But when *you* turn predator, that's another matter."

Jed thrust his thumbs into the waistband of his jeans. "All right. What are you talking about?"

Tor nodded at Marcie. "We'd like to be alone, sugar." She inclined her head and left. After she discreetly closed the door, Tor said, "I'm talking about Rob Malcolm."

"Rob Malcolm?" Jed sat down in the next swivel chair, cursing himself for being so obvious. "You're dreaming, Tor."

"She's an innocent, Jed."

Jed tenderly rubbed his bruised abdomen. "She's twenty-seven, and she's lived on a ranch her whole life. She's no innocent."

Tor raised one brow in the expression that had made his poster the highest seller of the year. "Really? Well, then, you won't mind if I whisper a word or two about life in her ear."

"You?" He almost snorted. "What could you possibly tell her?"

Tor grinned slyly. "Maybe enough to help her be the one woman who just might be able to make a fool of you."

No sooner had Jed left the makeup trailer for the set than he ran into Maxwell. Clearly this day wasn't going to get any better. Despite the 105-degree heat and the sand blowing into everything, the man was wearing a silk shirt and tie and a gray sharkskin suit, and he looked as pristine as if he had just stepped out of a fashion magazine.

"I want to talk to you about today's shooting, Jed. I have a few suggestions."

"Yeah?" Jed moved his director's chair into the boardwalk's shade and sprawled in the canvas seat.

Maxwell positioned another chair next to Jed's. "This scene is important. We have to grab the female audience with it, and the best way to do that is to go all the way with sexual tension."

Jed merely grunted. Rob Malcolm had stepped out of her dressing room and was heading for Makeup. The wind tousled her dark hair and whipped her long skirt around her, silhouetting the seductive line of her legs. There was an elusive quality about her, something unfinished. She had a face the cameras would love. And she had an uncanny ability to slip into the role of the Mexican Gypsy, if only she would let herself.

"I think we should start with one long static shot of Tor standing in front of the Gypsy girl's jacal," Maxwell was saying, "and then move right to the bed scene—close in on the girl stripping to her bare flesh, followed by the camera moving all around her and Tor writhing on her bed."

Jed picked up only on the words "her bare flesh." He fixed a lethal gaze on Maxwell. "I believe that I'm the director here. And *I'll* be the one to decide how we film this scene."

Peter Maxwell stared coolly back at him. "Now look, Jed, I'm not trying to take over. I'm just suggesting that our backers will be assured of a good return on their investment if we throw in enough flesh to make for good box office."

Something in Jed could not bring him to alter Rob's unnerving innocence and freshness. Nor did he want her character portrayed as an engine of seduction and destruction. "I guarantee you that the attraction will be hot enough between her and Tor to pack the movie houses, but we'll do it my way."

Maxwell arched a skeptical brow, but said only, "We'll wait to look at today's rushes before bringing in the verdict."

There was still an hour and a half before actual shooting got underway. Jed decided that Jack could lead the stand-ins through the camera and lighting re-

hearsal while he dealt with Rob. He was going to pre-
pare her for the love scene. No flesh. The sexual
tension had to be in her eyes, in her movements.

When he entered Makeup, Marcie glanced up with
a "you again?" expression, and Rob frowned at him
in the mirror. He had to get her to trust him. Under his
scrutiny, she shifted uneasily in her chair.

"Too much lipstick," he told Marcie, and snatched
a tissue from the box on the counter.

He swiveled Rob's chair around so that she was
facing him and grasped that imperious chin. Method-
ically he wiped the excess lipstick from her mouth. Her
mouth fascinated him. It was beautifully shaped, with
an ambiguous Pre-Raphaelite sensuality that contrasted with her no-nonsense eyes. But now her mouth
was set tautly, disapprovingly. He suspected that if her
arms hadn't been constrained by the plastic cape she
wore, she would have slapped his hand away.

He unsnapped the cape and caught her hands in his.
Her fingers were warm but stiff. Ignoring Marcie, he
said, "I want to go over the next scene with you. Come
on."

He half expected her to resist as he tugged her out
the door and back toward the trailer, but she didn't
pull back until he reached her door. "Why here?"

He opened the door and ushered her into her tiny
compartment. "Because," he said succinctly, "I want
to close us up in a room where we can tell each other
stories about sex." No use beating around the bush.

Rob was someone who was outspoken and appreciated the trait in others.

She retreated as far as the space allowed—one step—and was halted by the bathroom door. He had never been particularly aware of scents, but he could almost smell her fear. At her throat, her pulse pounded. "I don't know any stories about sex," she said thickly.

"But you have sexual thoughts, sexual feelings." He took her hand, chilled now, and drew her down onto the bench. She slid quickly to the far end. No more than two feet separated them. If he had wanted to, he could have captured a strand of her hair. It was so healthy, so shiny, so willful. Like her.

Eyes wide, she blurted, "I don't have any sexual feelings."

"Yes, you do. You're just not letting yourself call them up from the recesses of your mind. Surely," he said, his voice lowering, softening intimately, coaxing, "you have memories that have developed into fantasies."

"Fantasies?" Her voice was hardly more than a whisper.

How could he explain to her about fantasizing, something he so often resorted to when he bedded a woman because the women he knew were so boring. "Yeah. Like daydreaming about things that excite you. Excite you here." He reached and touched her low on her stomach, and he felt the muscles tighten beneath his fingertips.

"No," she breathed. "Nothing."

"I do." He let himself think back to one summer in particular. "I was on leave from the navy, and I'd missed a flight out of New York. So I hitchhiked to Pittsburgh, though God knows why. There was nothing and no one there for me to return to. Maybe just memories.

"Anyway, a woman in a convertible picked me up. I was skinnier than I am now. A young kid. All bones—except for my shoulders and arms. And the woman was in her early thirties, and gorgeous." His lids dropped to half-mast as he recalled that time. "She drove a red Porsche. I can still remember the purr of that convertible's engine. Power. And I can recall her perfectly. She was a striking blonde with opalescent skin. We cruised along for maybe thirty or forty miles. The August sun was burning down. She moved her hair away from her nape...stretched occasionally...raised her skirt above her knees... I dreamed that she didn't drop me off there on the interstate but took me to a motel. Took me to bed and taught me all that I didn't know about women and sex and loving."

Rob's face flushed with color. The small compartment was warm and isolating. Silence filled it with a thick presence, and he watched her strain to regain her composure under his unwavering gaze. She stared at him with a deliberately blank expression, a proud, closed look, but he could see the blood beating at her temples.

He took her hand again, his grip gentle, and traced the lines and ridges of old calluses and half-healed blisters and scars. His voice deepening, lazy and dark, he said, "Surely you can remember such an experience from your past."

"No." The denial barely cleared her throat.

He pushed back the wisps of dark hair that clung to her brow with perspiration. "I thought you were an honest person, Rob."

Her skin was taut over her chiseled cheekbones. Her clear, bottomless eyes were clouded with a confusion that he'd never seen there before. "I just can't think of anything...not when you're touching me like that."

His thumb ceased tracing its caressing concentric path over her palm, and he dropped his gaze to the small breasts that had visibly tightened beneath the flimsy cotton blouse. They were high and round, the skin satiny. He imagined the coral-colored nipples, and his throat constricted.

He wasn't used to having to wait for a woman he wanted. The thought startled him; he hadn't known he wanted her. Yet he knew at that moment that he had never wanted any woman the way he wanted this one.

"Try," he said quietly, hearing the rasp in his own voice.

"I am," she croaked. "I just can't remember—"

"Being interested in anyone of the opposite sex? Think about it. Think way back. Of something that was pleasurable that burned into your memory. And burned here." His fingers drifted back to her taut stomach, and he let them linger there, gently stroking in mist-light caresses. She closed her eyes, her lashes dark crescents above the erotic sweep of her cheekbones.

Because he was afraid he would begin to touch her all over, in places where she had never been touched, he forced his fingers to give up their sensual preoccupation. As a substitute, he captured her hand in his again. "Can you remember anything that gave you the good feeling you get when you're touched there?" he coaxed silkily.

Her eyes still closed, she breathed, "Yes. Sort of."

His gaze meandered down to her captivating mouth, softly parted now. He almost leaned forward to kiss those lips, but instead he contented himself with cupping her hand in his palm, contented himself with lightly rubbing his thumb over her knuckles. "Tell me."

She opened her eyes, and her irises were opaque now, moss-colored. "I can remember a hot summer afternoon, too. I was walking. My horse had thrown me and galloped back to the barn. Sweat was streaming down my...ribs." Unconsciously her hand drifted to the valley between her breasts. "I was maybe thirteen."

She paused, then went on in fragmented, wispy sentences. "I had cut across one of our pastures. There I was, trudging along, when I came up to the Wolf Creek tank. A strange horse was grazing there, and some guy was stretched out on the bank. He was lying faceup, hands locked behind his head, staring at the sky. And he wasn't wearing a shirt.''

She swallowed, glanced away, but continued in a thick voice. "I'd seen men without their shirts before, but somehow, this time... Anyway, the guy offered to take me back to the house. I can still remember riding behind him. I had my arms around his waist. I can remember the feel of his skin, hot and velvety and hard all at the same time.... And I can still remember the rhythm of his horse beneath me. A gorgeous horse. And the guy, too. 'Two studs' is the phrase that comes to my mind. It felt so good, riding behind him. It was a perfect afternoon. Everything was wonderful. The guy and the horse and the sun.''

She stopped, unaware that she was breathing shallowly, rapidly.

He had succeeded in seducing her into the state of mind required for the love scene. ''We're ready to film,'' he said abruptly.

But *he* wasn't ready. He wasn't ready to expose her to the prying eyes and leering thoughts of the others. He could close the set, could protect her privacy and her dormant passion from all but the most essential crew members, but he knew he couldn't protect her from himself.

Chapter 9

I haven't got time to fool with you, lady. Twenty-five dollars is my last offer."

Drops of water hung suspended from Tor's long, thick lashes. He stepped farther into the darkened jacal, and Rob moved back a step. The Gypsy mystique was a smoky aura around her. She wore the heavy gold ornaments and traditional long, swirling skirt. Her eyes taunted him.

"The horse is not mine to sell, *señor*." Her voice was low, breathless. The deep velvet of her eyes darkened as he moved in on her, and she didn't try to wrench her hand free from the grip that held it. Now her voice was steady, cool, but curiously full of satin sensuality. "Let go of me."

"Hell!" Frustrated fury glittered on that handsome face. His fingers released her hand, only to close around her throat. She froze, but her gaze held his. "If I can't have the horse...hell, why not!" he asked nastily.

His arm swept her against him, and his head bent to ravish her parted lips. She made a low, hungry sound in her throat, a savage, strangling noise. The kiss was a wild assault, full of exploding, irrational sensuality. His thighs opened to bring her into contact with his wet chaps and the pressure of his arousal.

When he lifted his head, his eyes looked as if they had turned to onyx. Her whole body trembled at his powerful closeness. Fury at being so easily taken narrowed her eyes into threatening slits. Her hand flailed wildly, chanced across the pearl handle of his pistol and jerked it from his holster. Swift as the snap of a whip, his hand knocked the pistol from her grip, and the shot went wild.

"You tried to kill me!" he snarled. His eyes glinted in disbelieving fury. His voice took on a heated promise as he said, "I'm going to return the deed in my own way. I'm going to go inside you, deep inside you, and listen to you moan."

Beneath his hot gaze, her own eyes smoldered with a sexual tension that was lethal. In an abrupt movement, he swung her onto her bed. She scrambled to the corner, braced for violence, but his fingers twined seductively in her hair. His kiss roamed angrily, commandingly, over her mouth, and she began to moan.

"For me, moan for me," he rasped, burying his face in the hollow of her neck.

Ecstasy played on her curved lips.

"You're a siren," he murmured. "You lured the horse out of the canyon to your side. You've lured me here. Now seduce me."

Her Gypsy eyes glowed with erotic intensity. She knelt on the mattress in front of him, her hands at her sides. Her lips grazed his softly in a tantalizingly prolonged kiss. He stood still, not even touching her now. A muscle ticked in his jaw.

The camera panned around them, slowly, then speeding up. The room whirled around them. At last she took her mouth from his. Her head thrown back, her lips parted in that intoxicating smile, she was the eternal woman.

Rob Malcolm didn't need elaborate dialogue. Her face told it all. She had the gift of economy in acting—and even in speech. Especially in speech.

The sound of the tail end of the film slapping against the projector indicated the end of the previous day's rushes. The lights flicked on in Marianna's office, which did duty at night as a projection room. It was full of smoke from Peter Maxwell's pipe, and the smell of the sophisticated cherry-blend tobacco irritated Jed's nostrils. He took a drag of his own cigarette, neglected until now because he had been diverted by Rob's riveting performance.

"Her acting's rough," Maxwell said.

"Yeah," Jed said, not at all perturbed. "She has an energy that liberates the film. She plays the roll with heat and bite."

"Jed, my friend, I think your brain is tangled up with your libido."

"She's real, damn it! She's not some plastic bimbo."

"You got the hots for her?"

How did he feel about her? He felt like more than a guardian, but sure as hell less than an angel. He took a swallow from an almost-empty bottle. The border beer was awful. He shot Maxwell a challenging stare. "She gets my vote. Consider it a take."

"The other backers see this clip and your screen-play is dog meat."

"Dog meat, you understand? You throw me again and I'll call the slaughterhouse. Got that?"

Death Threat eyed Rob suspiciously, then lowered his head, arched his back and bucked.

Somehow, before the filming of the final scene, in which the Gypsy girl and the wild horse united their wills to claim the rancher, she had to come to terms with Death Threat. One of them was going to come out of this the winner, and she meant for it to be her.

She didn't waste words cajoling Death Threat, or pat him encouragingly, or scratch his ears. None of that pleased the stallion. He was bad-tempered and moody from withers to tail. An unpredictable rogue, and clever. It was a battle of wills, and Death Threat knew it. The rogue stallion had indestructible courage, and she both admired and mistrusted him at the same time.

Those same feelings marked her attitude toward Jed Pulaski. She was powerfully drawn to him, and she didn't like that one bit. Yet she couldn't have gotten through filming the love scene yesterday afternoon without knowing that he was there, standing protectively between her and the few crew members necessary for filming. The wink he was in the habit of giving her just before a scene had encouraged her, but just barely. She'd had to trust him.

The worst was that she kept seeing Jed's face superimposed over the rancher's, over Tor's. It was Jed's gaze that had burned her with dark fire in her dressing room beforehand. He'd never looked at her quite that way before, and it had shaken her.

She might have spent her entire life on a ranch, but she was no fool. She knew that he wanted her, just as a stallion wants a mare. But Jed Pulaski rode his women hard. If she met him on his own ground, he would be more than she could handle.

She had only to look in the mirror, to listen to Marianna's pretty words, to observe Shyloh and Haydee in one of their women-to-women talks, to know that she wasn't woman enough to hold Jed. She was neither worldly-wise nor beautiful enough to keep this man who had seen it all.

"Give me a chance, Death Threat," she now said calmly to the horse.

urday afternoon, nearly a dozen people had showed
up in the ranch-house yard.

Jed had paperwork to catch up on but he had decided to accompany them. It wasn't that he had any
particular interest in watching a cockfight, but he *was*
eager to spend time with Rob, especially away from the
set.

The trip reminded him of an old-fashioned hay-
ride. Rob was driving her pickup, its bed strewn with
bits of straw. He could have chosen to ride with Rob
and Tor in the cab, but sheer perversity had prompted
him to let Linda drag him around to the tailgate. He
wanted to observe Rob's reaction. Would she care that
he wasn't riding with her? Was she indifferent to him
as a person? Certainly she wasn't indifferent to his
kisses, but that was something entirely different.

He was rewarded by the curious glance she cast his
way. Then, with a shrug, she slid behind the wheel.
Charley took the empty seat in front and crowded in
beside Tor, while the rest of the group crowded into
the back of the truck. The trip to Deming, the town
where the fight would be held, took about forty minutes. In the back of the pickup, everyone was drinking and joking and ignoring the scorching sun. Jed
was also ignoring Linda's attempts to flirt. To sleep
with him—hell, to sleep with any director—would be
a coup for her.

The cockfight turned out to be held near the mu-
nicipal airport. And no wonder. Small aircraft flew in
from all over for the occasion. Cockfighting might be

illegal in the United States, but New Mexico had never passed a state bill outlawing the centuries-old sport, so the New Mexico legislators simply turned their heads.

The cockfights were held in a large white building with a high ceiling. A heavy haze of smoke filled the place. Benches were set around a dirt arena where the spectators yelled either encouragement or their bets, frenziedly waving their money in their hands. At the sight of the smartly dressed film people, the arena went deadly still. Then Rob came into view. It was as if her presence sanctioned the others, and the clamor began again.

Most of the spectators were Hispanic. Jed noted that few were women, and all of those were Anglo. Most were clearly ranch women, tough, independent, weathered. He supposed that Rob would look weathered, too, as the years accumulated, but on her weathering would be an asset, bringing character lines that announced she was living her life as she wanted, without regard for public opinion. She was no hot-house lily, no clinging vine.

Although alcohol was supposedly prohibited inside the building, paper cups of straight tequila were more plentiful than popcorn at the movies. Charley elbowed him and held out a cup. Jed shook his head. These days, his predilection for the demon rum was waning without any conscious effort on his part. He supposed that filming in the great outdoors under such rigorous conditions was responsible.

As he took a seat, slightly behind Rob, a pair of roosters was brought into the roped-off ring. At the start of the fight the handlers held their birds firmly, allowing them to peck one another. When the roosters were angry enough, the handlers released them into the cockpit. Shouts of anticipation erupted from the audience as the two gamecocks dived at each other. A swirl of dust momentarily obscured the combatants, then settled to reveal the roosters furiously slashing each other with their spurs. Feathers flew. Blood splattered. They would fight until one died.

Excitement blazed in the spectators' faces. Jed studied them. For the Mexicans especially, this was clearly a sport as noble as horse racing or bull fighting.

For him it was no better, and no worse, than prize fighting.

Midway through the third match, he quietly excused himself. Outside, the sunshine and the pure air made him feel like a deep-sea diver surfacing. The noise from within was muted.

Leaning against the stucco wall, he tapped a cigarette from its package and lighted up. He could feel the soothing effects of the cigarette smoke eddying through him. He looked out over the high plains, trying to see the landscape as Rob Malcolm would. Brilliant emerald butterflies fluttered like miniature helicopters. Yellow coneflowers and delicate Indian paintbrush stubbornly survived.

"You all right?"

It was Rob, who had stepped around the corner of the building and was studying him with concern. She was wearing jeans that molded her lean racehorse frame. And the vulture-feathered hat was noticeably absent.

He smiled wryly. "I'm not squeamish, if that's what you mean."

She propped her back against the wall and crossed her arms over her chest. "No, I didn't think you were." When her head was turned toward him like that, the sunlight splintered in her eyes, dazzling him. "I just thought that . . . after having boxed, I mean . . . that all that fighting might have turned you off."

He hadn't analyzed his feelings, but now he realized that she was right. With her perceptiveness, she had picked up on his psychological turmoil. He studied her, amazed at how wise she was. Perhaps not wise about high finance or foreign relations, but wise in the things that mattered. "Do you come to these things often?"

"No, not these days, anyway. As a kid, I used to tag along with my father, the ranch hands, Tom—anyone who was going anywhere, even here. Those roosters . . . sometimes they aren't dead, Jed, when they're pitched in the trash barrel out back. Once I rescued one and begged one of the hands to let me bring it back to Mescalero. I nursed the rooster back to health."

"What happened to it?"

"Oh, one of the ranch hands wanted to put him into the cockpit again. I set him free the night before the fight."

How wonderful it was to watch Rob Malcolm! he thought. She was never afraid to see things as they were.

She looked askance at him. "Something wrong with me?"

He captured the braid draped over her shoulder. "No, something right." She looked puzzled, and he said quickly, "I'm interested in your opinion of what's going on in there."

She eyed him narrowly. "Why?"

"Because you always go straight to the heart of the matter."

She stared reflectively down at her boots, highly polished calfskin he noticed, not heavy clunkers that looked as if they'd been made for tramping through a pasture full of manure. "Well, when you first go in, everyone seems happy enough, relaxed and drinking. But when the fighting starts, they get all fired up and their faces began to look . . . oh . . . changing."

"Distorted?"

"Yes. Something earthy . . . ugly . . . within them begins to come to the top, and you can see it in their faces."

He smiled. She had pinpointed exactly what he had felt but hadn't been able to voice. Perhaps he had unconsciously been avoiding examining his feelings about boxing. He swung in front of her, his hands braced at either side of her, and leaned closer.

She stiffened. "What are you doing?"

"I'm not going to kiss you, if that's what you think," he said quietly, maintaining the half inch that separated their faces. He trailed his breath over her skin, blowing softly into her nostrils. "I'm bonding you to me."

She smiled slowly, and his heart seemed to jump. He was light-headed with wanting her. "They say a horse doesn't really know you till you've shared breath with it," she murmured.

"Then share your breath with me, Rob."

Her skin flushed with either pleasure or alarm, he wasn't certain which. He waited for a long, agonizing moment. Then she parted her lips and gently exhaled. Her breath was sweet, like fresh grass, without the smell of cigarettes or liquor. And her skin was fresh, with no lingering stale-perfume scent. A scorching hunger filled his body. "Again," he said.

But this time he lowered his mouth over hers, catching her breath. His blood surged like a high tide under the full moon, powerful, disturbing.

"So there you are," Tor said, coming around the corner. Then he spotted Rob, hidden by Jed's big body, and said, "Whoops, sorry. Didn't mean to intrude."

But Jed had the distinct impression that that was exactly what Tor O'Donnel had intended. The handsome actor was making a valiant effort to save Rob from the notorious womanizer.

Landis scrutinized her face in the bedroom's full-length mirror. Her lips were mapped with tiny seams. Her flesh looked overexposed and bruised. And her face had enough laugh lines on it to indicate that she should have been amused for almost five decades.

She glanced at the dress, a violet designer original that was at least a size too small for her. Perhaps a bit *de trop*, too expensive for dinner at a ranch house. But she had to sway Jed to her side. That Malcolm girl was getting too much screen time. Landis couldn't quite put her finger on it, but the ranch woman was undergoing some kind of extraordinary erotic transformation. She positively glowed.

Slowly Landis pirouetted in front of the mirror, then raked her fingers through her hair, tossed back her head and wet her lips.

What's that girl got that I haven't? she asked herself. But she knew the answer all too well.

Youth.

So what if Rob Malcolm was young? So what if she was Venus on the half shell, dewy and expectant? One day she would be thick-waisted, heavy, broad of beam.

While I am a nicely proportioned size 8, she told herself. And starving.

She glanced back at the mirror for what she hoped would be a reassuring look. Instead, she began to

undo her zipper. Oh, well, the dress was no great
shakes anyway.

By the time she descended to the dining room,
everyone was seated at the table, chatting and passing
platters laden with food. She had staged her late entrance on purpose, but what she hadn't planned on
was being put at one end of the table, with Jed at the
other. Usually they sat in the same vicinity, but the
only vacant chair was between that obnoxious cow-
poke, Emmitt, and Red Eye. A huge table, and she
had to end up between two twits.

The old Indian fixed her with one of his unnerving
eagle-eyed glares. He nodded his head judiciously.
"You got sand." His breath was a trumpet blast of
cheap whiskey.

"I beg your pardon?"

"Grit, ma'am," Emmitt said. "Sand is grit. You
know, guts."

"I see," she managed, then glanced down toward
the other end of the table, where Peter Maxwell was
talking in his usual smooth manner.

"...no way to tell what the public wants. Producers can watch the trade papers' reports of grosses, but
the numbers for one film can never predict how
the..."

She slid her gaze over to Jed to try to determine just
how receptive he might be to suggestions from her. He
appeared to be listening to Peter, but his dark gaze was
on Rob. With something akin to amazement, Landis
saw not the usual indifference reflected in Jed's eyes

but a smoldering look that outburned the candles in the center of the table.

Landis peered critically at the object of Jed's desire. Why, if you really studied the young woman, it was obvious that she was almost plain.

Dear God, how long before this dinner was over? she asked herself when dessert was served. She couldn't stand it another minute. "I'm going outside for a cigarette," she murmured.

Her departure went unnoticed by the rest of the guests. She slipped out the front door and, dropping down onto the veranda swing, sighed wearily. "What a menagerie!" she muttered, and dug around in her small purse for her cigarettes.

Twenty minutes later, she ground out her third cigarette on the veranda's plank floor. She needed to corner Jed.

Back in the dining room, a few people still lingered around the dining table, but Jed wasn't one of them. He could have turned in already, or maybe he was with Peter in the makeshift projection room.

Her indecision must have shown, because the older son—a good-looking young man, she noted, not for the first time—said, "You looking for Jed? He headed out toward the gazebo a few minutes ago."

"Thanks." She gave Rand one of her perfunctorily seductive smiles and headed back outside, her smile fading. Jed was undoubtedly with Rob. The girl had gotten to him first!

But Landis hadn't survived in Hollywood, the worst sort of civilized jungle, solely because of her charm. Cunning had helped her along the way. Now she knew she would just have to get serious.

Chapter 10

He had to make her forget where she was, where she had grown up. He had to make her see him as just a man, and herself as just a woman.

Perhaps Maxwell had been right about him and his feelings for Rob.

All his life, it seemed, he had been on an odyssey, searching for life's meaning, for a place that so far existed only in his imagination—mythical and beautiful, staggering the senses with its quiet power and its peace, wiping out the desire to run because it offered freedom.

And he wanted Rob to be his companion on that journey.

He took her hand and pulled her down beside him on the wide bench that followed the perimeter of the gazebo. She acquiesced, but there was a speculative look in her hazel eyes. He simply held her hand, their clasped hands resting on his taut thigh. Her hand was strong, real. Not for her the smothering softness of the glitter girls he had grown so tired of.

For the moment he was content to enjoy the quiet of the desert night. Rob, too, appreciated its stillness. Her silence was soothing, penetrating his shell to reach the vulnerable man inside.

It was amazing how the high desert could be boiling by daylight, yet cool so rapidly in the depth of the night. The air might be chilly, but in the dense black sky, the stars were hot. And bright. Billions of them. Rather than feeling diminished by their infinite number, he felt an enormous assurance of his place in such a grand scheme.

"In places like Los Angeles and Chicago and Pittsburgh," he murmured, more to himself than her, "you don't see the stars. Not really see them, and you tend to lose all sense of what's important, all perspective."

A hunting owl floated past to disturb the silence, and a coyote yipped in the pasture beyond. Rob's hand stirred in his, freeing itself, and he asked, "You aren't afraid, are you?"

Her laugh was low, throaty. Nothing dainty about her, he thought. She was as strong as the land, strong with the security of her convictions. "Nope. Hearing the coyotes makes me feel restless, makes me want to up and join them, to run wild across the desert." She shifted, unconsciously leaning into him. "Look, see the falling star?"

"A meteor," he murmured prosaically, distracted by the brush of her pouty breasts against his chest.

"Did you know that if you really watch the stars you can make out dozens of satellites moving across the heavens?"

"No, I didn't." She longed to run wild, he thought. Would he be her cage?

"I sometimes resent their presence. Cold machines, stealing their light from the sun. Man-made eyes and ears that leave nowhere for a person to find herself."

His fingers were tempted by the rawhide lace that bound her luxuriant hair. "I have the feeling that you never lose yourself." He gave in to desire and tugged on the rawhide strip.

From beneath the thick fringe of her dark lashes, she eyed him cautiously. "I do." Her voice was husky. "When I'm with you."

His fingers wove through her heavy braid until her hair fell free to mantle her strong shoulders. "Why?" He had to know. He had to understand this woman who had so disrupted his life.

Impatiently she shook her head, and her hair glided silkily over the inner skin of his wrist. "I don't know. I wish I did." Suddenly her eyes took on the clarity of green crystals. "It's like what you said about big cities and how you lose all perspective when you can't see the stars. With you, I lose all perspective."

Extraordinary, how articulate she was. She was well
balanced and sane in a world spinning out of control.
He couldn't help himself. With unhurried grace, he
bent toward her. "What happens?"

"Heat," she murmured. "It spreads in me, in my
stomach. And I can't think clearly. My mind gets all
hazy."

His thumb followed the supple line of her throat. At
its base, he found her pulse throbbing in the hollow
formed at the juncture of her collarbone. The ends of
the rawhide string, clutched within his palm, swayed
against the tantalizing flesh exposed by the opening of
her gingham shirt and dipped inside.

She pressed herself backward against the gazebo's
white-painted latticework. Slivers of moonlight di-
vulged the heightened color that stung her cheeks.

He took the rawhide and looped it over her wrist.
"Don't think," he said, drawing her back to him, inch
by inch. The scent of her overwhelmed him, unlike the
sophisticated scents of expensive perfumes that only
blunted the senses. He felt as if he had just finished
running a marathon—light-headed, weak-kneed and
breathless. And there was another feeling—raw hunger. As if he had been starving all his life.

In an attempt to escape, she pushed blindly against
the solid muscle of his thigh...and her hand remained there, lightly, ready to fly away at any threat.
"You'll empty me."

"Yes." It was said only on a breath, as a warning.
A shadow of sadness touched his soul. Still holding

her imprisoned with the thin length of rawhide, he brushed the back of his other hand down the satiny V of her chest, halting at its rising slope.

"I should run now," she said, lips parted, eyes closed against the strength of his physical image. "While I still can."

"Yes. But I don't think you will. Your kind never run from life, my beautiful wild creature."

She moved slightly, and the moonlight drenched her sculpted face. Her eyes drifted open, and a sorrowful smile played at the corners of her wide, marvelous mouth. "No, but long after you've used me up and forgotten me, you'll still be searching for something to fill your emptiness."

Of all the things she could have said, this insightful statement took him completely by surprise. A new emotion stabbed him, something so elusive that it was gone before he could identify it.

"I guess you think I'm something of a trophy hunter," he said with dark irony. "Well, you've been forewarned, Rob."

Lazily his hand splayed over the gentle mound of her breast, and her breath quickened in an almost inaudible gasp that made his blood race. Against his palm he felt the tightening of an insistent nipple. He was so tempted. She struck more than a chord in him, she struck the whole damn keyboard.

But he resisted his inner upheaval and directed himself toward his primary object. "You know we halt shooting at Mescalero the day after tomorrow. Tor's contract calls for a two-week leave of absence so he can film a television special.''

It was merely a sigh she gave, no more than the smallest breath, but he knew then that he had the edge. ''You'll have to leave here, you know,'' he said softly.

Her eyes flared, her body shrank from him. ''Leave Mescalero?''

He tugged on the rawhide loop around her wrist, drawing her close again. He slid a finger between her blouse's top two buttons, bewitchingly stroking the soft skin of the valley between those small but perfectly formed breasts. Reluctantly he drew his gaze away. ''Yes. We have to go to Ixtapa—on Mexico's Pacific coast. To shoot the first twelve scenes.''

Distress edged her voice. ''You didn't tell me I'd have to leave when I agreed to take over the part.''

''It's in the contract. Besides, it's just for two weeks.''

''But Mexico, it's . . . so far!''

''As I recall, it's only about twenty miles south.''

''Can't we change the contract?'' she asked. ''Talk to the woman at your Malibu house.''

''What?''

''The wardrobe mistress, I overheard her say that the woman . . . sleeping with you . . . was a lawyer. An entertainment lawyer.''

''She doesn't sleep with me, Rob.''

''I'm not a city animal, Jed. I can't go! All that concrete would corral me!''

"How do you know until you give it a try?"

He freed her top button. The rapid rise and fall of her breasts startled him. The skin that had never seen sunlight contrasted so starkly with the tanned skin of her throat. He hadn't realized that makeup had camouflaged the flesh exposed by the low-cut Gypsy blouse. "Don't you feel safe with me?"

"No. No, it's not that." She was so distraught that she made no move to cover herself. She only shook her head slowly. "No, with you I know the danger."

He grimaced. "Not exactly a compliment, is it?"

"I—I just don't want to go."

"You want that cutting-horse ranch, right?"

She tilted her head to look at him. The naked desolation in her eyes astonished him. "You come prepared to win the blue ribbon at all costs, don't you?"

He captured her face between his hands. "Listen, Rob, there's practically nothing you wouldn't do to have that ranch of yours, right? You'd work like hell. That's how I feel about this film. It's more than just a way to make money. It's a part of me. If I succeed with *Sierra Sundown*, it means that I've left something lasting, that I'm not just a hack."

She twisted free of him and rose with the unschooled grace that was so natural to her, her eyes sad. "You said it all, Jed. There's *practically* nothing I wouldn't do to get my ranch. But you...you'd do anything."

He shot to his feet, anger surging through his veins. "You're damned right, Rob! I was raised on the streets, where you either have that winning edge or you end up facedown in a gutter. All your life you've hidden out here at Mescalero, safe and protected. You don't know a damn thing about fear, about loneliness. Now, are you going to Mexico with me or not?''

"Yes," she said dully. "I'll go."

He didn't feel the elation he should have. "Should I talk to Tom and arrange matters?''

She shook her head, and her waist-length hair slid over her shoulders to hide her breasts. "No. Like I told you before, I'm my own woman."

He knew that all too well.

He'd been away from the reservation too long, and a part of him, no matter how much he clung to the Indian traditions, had begun to think like a white man. Colt bent, retrieved the stale cigarette he had ground out in the dust with his boot and shredded it, so that nothing was left to contaminate the Earth Mother.

The moon was still out, although the sun would shortly rise. Using the moonlight, he made an examination of the barn and corral. The dust held what he was looking for. The Indian in him could track the morning mist. He dropped to one knee and lightly ran a sensitive fingertip around one recent imprint. The shape of the boot, its right heel slightly worn at the edge, and the depth of the imprint around the sole's outer curves gave him his answer. Doyle Reese. The man had been here just as the dew had been beginning to glaze the land.

The rancher's late-night visit accounted for the wild snorting and the crashing of hooves against wood that had woken Colt. Death Threat was temperamental, but not a frenzied killer—at least not until Reese appeared. The horse hated even the smell of the man, and the man cared nothing about the animal, only about the money it would bring in from the film deal.

Furious, almost demented nickering drew Colt inside the immense barn. In another half hour the ranch would be alive, the hands drifting down to the barn, yawning and stretching and cursing good-naturedly. But now Colt was the only man there, and he had work to do. In the far stall, Death Threat threw up his head, his teeth bared and his eyes distended.

"Easy there," Colt said in a voice as soothing as that of old Fred Fourth. The aged Apache medicine man had been grooming him for years to take his place as medicine man on the Mescalero Indian Reservation, to invoke the spirits needed for healing or blessings.

One glance at the snorting Death Threat and Colt reckoned Rob was going to need a blessing if Jed Pulaski planned to have her ride that beast today. The scene, as Rob had related it last night, called for the Gypsy girl to ride the stallion and lead its band of mares through the frontier town at the same moment that Tor's character was to be lynched by the bloodthirsty citizens.

Rob, who had an affinity for horses, could wrangle and ride as well as any man, but hampered by the skirts she would be wearing for today's scene...he knew his aunt would have her work cut out for her in trying to ride Death Threat.

Carefully he opened the stall door and entered on quiet moccasined feet, closing the door behind him but not latching it. Death Threat neighed threateningly and pawed the sawdust. Colt ducked as the horse rose on its hind legs then came up on the stallion's far side. When the flying hooves pounded into the sawdust, he quickly slid onto the animal's back, Indianstyle. Taken by surprise, Death Threat went momentarily rigid. Colt took advantage of the horse's dismay and leaned forward to shove open the stall door. That slight movement almost cost him his seat, because the furious animal bolted out of the barn and along the chute.

It got no farther than the first pen. Its flight blocked, it went into a frenzy of bucking and twisting and diving. His hand knotted in Death Threat's mane, Colt stayed with the rampaging horse, but just barely, which told him something about the extraordinary strength of the crazed animal.

Despite the predawn coolness, foam flecked the horse's mouth and sweat steamed off its flanks, but it slowed its mad dance. Rivulets of perspiration ran down Colt's chest and rib cage. "I'm going to ride you to hell this morning. Then you're gonna be a damned sight easier on Rob this afternoon or I'll make pemmican out of you. Understand, cayuse?"

Though he had spoken almost inaudibly, more to himself than the horse, and in Apache, he felt certain the animal had understood his threat quite well.

Tom had taught him how to bust broncos, and rodeo prize money had provided him with tuition and books at State, so he knew his horses, and this one had more tainting it than just a fiery temper and a master with a mean streak. The docile way it momentarily hung its head, as if acknowledging that it had lost, didn't fool Colt for one moment. Between his thighs he could feel the animal gathering its strength for another explosion of fury. Rob wouldn't have stood a chance this afternoon.

"You did it, Colt!"

In the predawn darkness, Shyloh, laughing joyously, sprinted from a mesquite's darker shadows across the yard toward him. Her hair, the color of winter moonlight, streamed behind her. He should have realized her intentions, but the sight of her nightgown, hitched up above her knees, momentarily distracted him.

"You were magnificent!" she said, sliding between two of the corral's slats.

"No, Shy—"

Before the words of warning left his tongue, she had hurried to him, her hand clasping his knee, her face upturned, the affection in her eyes piercing him.

At that moment Death Threat unleashed his suppressed rage. He reared almost perpendicularly, concentrating all his brute force in the slashing descent of his vicious hooves. In the space of an eternal second, Shyloh screamed, shielded her face with her arms and stumbled backward, trying to dodge almost certain death. With all his strength, fueled by instant adrenaline, Colt sawed brutally on the horse's mane, throwing his weight to the far side to draw Death Threat off balance. A thousand pounds of horseflesh slammed against the ground, and the crushing impact wired the nerves in Colt's right leg with ten thousand volts of pain.

Jed Pulaski drank hard, but he rarely showed the effects of veins flowing with 90-proof. His drinking would kill him one day, Tom thought, but that wasn't his problem.

Rob *was* his problem. His sister was too headstrong, and he worried about her. Maybe some of his worrying was a result of guilt. He had always told himself that he had done the best he could to raise her, but there had always been hassles to iron out, a thousand details to resolve. As a result, Rob had grown up on her own, without the benefit of a woman's guidance. He might have taught her to handle herself well in her own environment, but in an unfamiliar setting—?

He knocked on Jed's bedroom door. Jed, shirtless, opened the door, then grinned sardonically. "Been expecting you, Malcolm." He stood aside and motioned for Tom to enter. On the bed was an expensive leather suitcase, opened and partially packed. Jed turned his back to toss a pair of jeans inside.

"Then you know I've come about Rob," Tom said, crossing to the window. He stood looking out at the south pasture, where the yearlings grazed in the red haze of sunset. His hands were thrust into the back pockets of his jeans because he wasn't sure he could look Jed in the face without wanting to hit him. And Tom knew he was the last one who should be doing any sanctimonious punching. Hadn't his intentions toward Marianna been less than honorable at the beginning?

"Rob's a grown woman," Jed said behind him. "Her own woman, to use her words."

"But I'm still her brother."

Tom turned back to the man. Jed was taking a package of cigarettes from his shirt pocket. He offered one to Tom, who shook his head. Instead, he drew a cigar out of his own shirt pocket and jammed it between his teeth without bothering to light it.

Jed eased into a wooden fan-back chair on the far side of the bed and propped one ankle across the opposite knee. Smoke drifted from his lips as he stared back at Tom. Finally he said, "I'm...interested in your sister."

Tom bit down on his cigar. "Does that mean you're infatuated with her, or does that mean you love her?"

"I don't know," Jed said bluntly. "I'm still finding out."

"Well, I don't want your self-discovery to be at the cost of my sister. Understand me?"

"Your wife and I have more in common than film-making. Did you know that?"

The abrupt shift of subject took Tom by surprise. "Is this relevant, Pulaski?"

"We've both done time in prison," Jed went on without answering Tom's question. "Did about the same amount of time—six weeks, in my case. Except . . . I was convicted of murdering a man."

"Did you do it?"

"Yes, in a way." A terrible haunted look came into his eyes. "I won't go into the details. The point is, your wife and I both know the value of freedom. It can be intoxicating to those who live with the memory of losing it. Once you escape that cell, everything is brand-new to you—the sounds, the smells, the sights. It's like being dropped from another civilization. The stars, a sunrise or a sunset . . . they acquire immense, intense importance. Freedom becomes invaluable."

Tom chewed thoughtfully on his cigar. "Does Rob understand that you won't surrender yours?"

"How could she?" Jed stared pointedly at him. "She doesn't know that she's imprisoned, so how could she understand a concept like the loss of freedom?"

"Imprisoned?" Tom felt defensive anger boiling up in him.

"Yeah," Jed grunted. "Imprisoned. She's been raised in a male-oriented, male-dominated society. She's never tasted the world, so she doesn't know whether what's being withheld from her is important or not."

"Withheld!" Realizing that he had practically shouted the word, Tom softened his voice. "Listen to me, Pulaski. Anything I had, which at times wasn't much, was always one-half Rob's."

"But are you going to let her try her wings, Malcolm? Are you going to open that cage door?" Jed rose. "And when it comes down to it, whatever you decide doesn't matter one damn bit, because in the end Rob will do exactly what she wants. You know that better than anyone." He gave a deprecatory grimace. "I can only promise you that I'll do my best to see that she doesn't get hurt."

Marianna watched Shyloh carry a glass of champagne punch to Colt, who sat in the large leather chair, his broken leg propped on the matching ottoman, his crutches balanced against the nearby wall. The other revelers in the balloon-decked and streamer-draped main room were laughing and joking and didn't notice the abject misery in Shyloh's eyes. And even if the others had noticed it and then guessed its source, her guilt at being the cause of Colt's injury, they would never have suspected the joy that lurked just behind that misery... would never have guessed that Shyloh, like New Mexico's legendary *penitentes*, scourged herself and rejoiced in her suffering. In serving Colt, she was the nearest she could ever hope to be to paradise.

Marianna's gaze slid to Colt. He was oblivious of Shyloh's adulation, an adulation that would surely evolve into love. Marianna had known for some time now that eventually she would have to send Shyloh away.

The sound of spurs jangling on the stairs turned Marianna's attention to her husband, who was followed by Jed Pulaski. She had no doubt as to what had been going on upstairs. A showdown. Once, when she had first arrived at Mescalero, Tom had accused her of being overly protective of Shyloh, of mother-henning her because of her heart murmur. Well, now Tom was learning the painful process of letting go. Her heart ached for him.

He hunkered down on one knee in front of Colt. "How long did the doctor say you'd be out of commission, boy?"

Colt's dark eyes narrowed. In spite of his stoic impassiveness, Marianna knew that he longed for his father to call him *son*. Just once. "Two or three months."

Tom nodded and laid an affectionate hand on Colt's plaster cast. Then he stood, towering over everyone else in the big room. His thick brows were lowered over smoldering eyes as he assessed the damage to his secondborn son. "I've got a mind to shoot that horse of Reese's."

"No," Jed said.

Marianna looked askance at him. No one ever contradicted Tom. Well, no one but herself. And even then, never within earshot of the ranch hands.

Jed ambled over to where Rob was perched on a bar stool. "The first day I arrived, your sister taught me that you don't shoot wild things."

Marianna didn't miss the look Rob cast Jed. Her sister-in-law, Marianna sensed, was in over her head and would need all her strength in the weeks ahead.

Pushing away her concern for her loved ones, Marianna donned her best smile, a truly genuine one. "I have an announcement," she said.

The murmur of conversation ebbed in expectation. She wouldn't disappoint her guests. Crossing to Tom, she linked her arm in his and smiled up at him tenderly. "Tom and I are going to have a baby."

Bliss flowed through her, and she leaned into the curve of the mighty arm he wrapped around her.

I must cherish this moment against the hard times ahead, she thought, sorrow mixing with her joy.

Chapter 11

With its millions of inhabitants, Mexico City was the second largest city in the world. The taxi zipped in and out of the traffic that surged along the tree-lined Paseo de la Reforma. The midmorning sunshine, though hot, was fuzzy with smog. Already Rob missed the pristine air of New Mexico.

Suddenly the taxi roared into the plaza circling the monument called El Angel, throwing her against Jed. She didn't fight the arm that banded her, anchoring her. In fact, she was reluctantly grateful. With a horse beneath her, she could pick up the signaling vibrations from its muscles before it ever made a turn, but an automobile gave no such warning.

She hadn't liked the airplane, either. Inside it, she had had no control over her fate. Worse than that, she had felt fenced in. How did prisoners survive? How had Marianna managed it?

The taxi swerved onto Calle Londres, then screeched to a halt in front of the Zona Rosa's exclusive Hotel El Dorado. A doorman in royal-purple livery hurried from beneath the maroon-striped canopy to commandeer the luggage. Inside the El Dorado, she at once felt overpowered by its glass and greenery and gold. She stared in wonder at her hundredfold reflection in the mirror-lined lobby. In her denim jacket and skirt—a concession to Marianna—she looked out of place among the chic jet-setters loitering over frothy fruit drinks and brunch on the lobby's vine-draped patio.

A plastic card inserted in the elevator panel magically and silently carried her and Jed to the penthouse floor. So this was what it felt like to ride on a magic missile. "The bedrooms..." she began.

Jed looked pained beyond endurance. "... are separate. The baths, too. Give me credit for more finesse than that, Rob."

Disconcerted, she kept her gaze on the swiftly changing floor numbers. When the elevator stopped, she stepped out, stopped and glanced around. Polished marble and glass; deep sofas and chairs of lush velvet; a terrace with a panoramic view of the city's unbridled development, which was rapidly overtaking the mountains beyond.

"Well?" Jed drawled.

She fumbled for a word that could explain what she was feeling. She came up with the precise one. "Insignificant. All this makes me feel insignificant."

He cast her a marveling look, then crossed to the mirror-paneled bar and took down two shot glasses. The mirror reflected his hard good looks, and she tried to stop gaping at his reckless mouth, strongly carved cheekbones, chiseled nose and fascinating eyes. "I know," he was saying. "I feel the same way when I look at your vast, empty desert."

For the first time since boarding the plane at El Paso's international airport, she smiled. "But in my desert you can feel a sense of yourself. 'You are a child of the universe, no less than the trees or the stars. You have a right to be here.' Or something like that."

He set down the crystal decanter of Scotch and stared at her. She had sensed that she would have to win him by meeting him on his own level, and his face reflected what she had been seeking from him: approval. "Where did you hear that?"

She shrugged, but it was hard not to puff up like a pigeon. "I've been studying."

Almost every night, in fact. It didn't matter if filming finished at two in the morning; she tried to keep her eyes open long enough to get in at least half an hour of reading books purloined from Tom's office. Why had he felt the need to get a college education, yet she hadn't? She knew she had a good mind. And her brother, as well as Marianna, had certainly urged her over the years to take some college courses. But she'd been content there at Mescalero.

Had been.

"Come here," Jed said softly.

His eyes held hers as she crossed the plush carpet. When she halted before the bar, he reached out and ran a thumb along her hairline, almost wonderingly. At his touch, she trembled, like an aspen rustled by a mountain breeze. "You're unlike any woman I've ever known."

She wanted to ask how many women he had known. But she merely accepted the glass he passed to her, asking instead, "What is it?"

"Perrier. Chilled mineral water." He took a deep draft of his own Scotch, grunted with satisfaction, then said, "It's a good thing you don't drink, because you're going to need all your wits about you tomorrow night when you face the media."

Her lungs shut down. "I'm going to be interviewed?"

"You're going to be dissected, probed and turned inside out. And tomorrow's only the beginning. When the film is released, you'll be besieged by journalists, I promise you."

She could feel the blood draining from her face, taking its heat with it. "Jed, I only made one speech in high school, and I made a prize fool of myself. Stammering and forgetting and turning beet red."

"I'll be there to run interference, sweetheart." The tough edge to his smile was reassuring. "And I've prepared a game plan that we'll carry out before you ever hit the conference room downstairs.''

His game plan was almost as arduous as a day of hay baling. With bewildering speed, he shuttled her from one haute couture house to another in the Pink Zone. Dapper clerks, polite assistants in sober suits and obsequious saleswomen labored over her while Jed, like some Middle Eastern potentate, oversaw the process. The slightest shake of his head and the offending outfit was instantly removed. At the jewelry houses she was adorned with glittering gems.

"Who pays for all this?" she asked as Jed arranged to have a battery of designer boxes delivered to their hotel.

Jed's eyes twinkled. "Maxwell will have an embolism when he sees the bills. But the designer clothing and beautiful baubles will merely insure that his partners get a tidy return on their investment."

Silk dresses, satin gowns, crinolines that looked like roses in full bloom. She changed costumes so many times that she lost count. For the next day's press conference, Jed settled on a tailored jacket and skirt that the debonair shopkeeper called "sophisticated suede."

"It suits you," Jed said approvingly of the rich rust-colored outfit. "Suede boots, a cream silk blouse and that heavy gold necklace ought to complete the effect."

She stared at her reflection, unable to believe that the stunning young woman who pivoted and sauntered and posed was really her, then she turned back to Jed and with a wistful smile said, "'Fashion is what one wears oneself, what is unfashionable is what other people wear.' Isn't that what Oscar Wilde said?"

He grinned. "That's one for you, sweetheart."

"The hair, *señor*?" one shopkeeper asked with a suggestive wave of his hand. "Perhaps a stylish cut to emphasize the broad cheek—"

"No," Jed said flatly. "I don't want a mannequin."

When they returned to the hotel, she found their sitting room cluttered with boxes. "Such a waste," she said.

She turned to find Jed, fists on hips, watching her from the vestibule. His eyes flared, as if he couldn't quite believe her. She had the strong desire to go to him, to seek shelter in his arms from the after-effects of this bewildering day. But she remembered him telling her that, day by day, everyone surrendered parts of themselves. She had a terrible feeling in her bones that if she gave up even a small part of herself to him, all of her would be lost. He would overwhelm her. He did that to people. She murmured, "I'll never wear all this."

"It is a waste," he said, his eyes raking over her in a measuring way. "Because I imagine you're one of the few women who look absolutely perfect without clothes. Square shoulders, slim hips, long, well-proportioned legs. Hell, I don't have to imagine it. But I do. Every night."

She could hear the wanting in his voice. And, hearing it, she felt a disturbing combination of pleasure and alarm.

"I imagine what it would be like to be loved by a woman who places a value on love," he continued in that mesmerizing voice of his. "And I think about what I could bring to her. More than simple pleasure. No, just as this woman would have the power to make me constantly want her, I would have that same power over her, the power to bring her desires to the boiling point."

He had aroused the woman in her, and she didn't know how to handle it. Her nipples involuntarily contracted into aching buds, and excitement knotted painfully deep between her thighs. Her throat was tight with emotion, and she stared back at him mutely.

"I've got some calls to make," he said brusquely, and headed for the telephone. "Why don't you take a hot, relaxing bath? Then we'll get something to eat before the party."

"Party?"

"A little shindig put on by the studio's Mexican distributors." He picked up the receiver and began dialing. "The apricot gown will do. Operator, put this on my credit-card number...."

Released from his spell, she made her way to her own private bathroom.

The warm, scented water was wonderful, and she had to smile, thinking of the times as a child when she had had to shower in cold water because there hadn't been sufficient propane. A life like this could grow on you. It could also weaken you. She sprang from the tub and began to dry herself vigorously with one of the large, thick towels the hotel had provided. Then she dressed in one of her new evening gowns. Didn't people who lived this kind of life begin to feel useless?

Rather than do her hair, she wound the braid atop her head. A feeling of restraint was needed somewhere, she thought ruefully, so why not her hair? The apricot dress certainly didn't offer much along that line. Floor-length, it was dramatically draped from one shoulder, reminding her of a Roman toga. The elegant gold crescent necklace set off the simple flow of the gown.

Jed nodded his approval when she entered the sitting room, his eyes glittering with amber sparks. He tossed down his drink and muttered, "Professor Higgins would certainly appreciate the transformation."

"What?" She should have been paying more attention, but the sight of Jed in his black dinner jacket had caught her unawares. The black bow tie, the small ruffled pleats on the white shirt, the gold chunks adorning each cuff—he looked like one of the society photos in the Sunday edition of the El Paso newspaper.

No, that wasn't true. His battle-scarred face, handsome in its own arrogant way, his broad shoulders and tapering hips, saved him from looking like a dandified politician, she thought. Jed Pulaski was the most intimidating man she'd ever come across. Elegant yet rough. Educated but streetwise. Soft-spoken yet dangerous.

"Nothing." He shook his head, as if shaking off the effects of too much wine, and said, "We're running late, but then, you're the star and entitled to make a grand entrance."

Star? Surely not her. Not Rob Malcolm, the six-foot girl wonder who'd never had a date in high school. Not that she'd really cared.

The party was held in the fashionable Lomas section of Mexico City, at the palatial home of one of the studio's branch executives. The hacienda-style mansion was set behind high stucco walls at the end of a long graveled drive.

A black-uniformed maid ushered them along a tiled corridor and out into an immense yard that Rob decided had more trees than all of southeast New Mexico combined. Wrought-iron lanterns spread a soft yellow glow over the manicured lawn. Her eyes widened at the sight of pink flamingos daintily picking their way over the lush grass. The night was balmy, and a hundred people or more, drinks in hand, were milling around like restless cattle. Some had queued up at a table draped with white linen and mounded with food more colorful than a box of crayons.

The hostess, an older woman wearing a lot of makeup, bore down on Jed. "Darling, it's about time. But you never were one to comply with convention." She kissed him soundly on the lips, and Rob stared, astounded. The woman was old enough to be his mother. Then the woman turned to her. "So this is your latest protégée."

Protégée? Rob glanced at Jed for an explanation. His eyes narrowed, but he answered mildly, "It means you're under my protection, Rob."

"How droll!" the hostess said. Except for the glance she had spared Rob, she had yet to take her eyes off Jed. "Do come along and meet everyone."

Rob found the touch of Jed's hand at her elbow reassuring. He steered her among guests who called out to him and eyed her speculatively. Here and there he made introductions. She kept her remarks to a minimum, afraid of coming out with something that would raise eyebrows. She didn't want to embarrass Jed.

A drink was pressed on her. She would rather have had food, and she started to ask Jed if they could go over to the table where two Mexican waiters were serving dinner. But a blonde in a slinky red gown drew Jed aside, cornering him beneath some kind of tropical tree.

Rob shrugged and headed for the table. Hers wasn't a sparrow's appetite, and she stared in disappointment at the bite-size food on the trays—canapés, she guessed, like the ones Haydee prepared, but all foreign-looking.

"You know, you're not supposed to eat vegetables raw here," a young man said beside her. He was dressed in a conservative black dinner jacket, but his hair was spiked and dyed purple. He grinned outrageously and offered her some kind of toast topped with black stuff.

So this was Jed's culture. Its newness was quickly wearing off. She shook her head and moved farther along the table. Someone else, a middle-aged man who looked normal compared to the joker behind her, winked and said, "Word's out that you're a cowgirl turned actress."

She nodded and kept moving. Her plate was still empty, but nothing looked appetizing.

"Tell me," he said, giving her a confidential smile, "Was Freud right? Does riding horses really give you a thrill?"

She stared at him in disbelief. This was polite society?

She turned to search for Jed. He was making his way toward her, politely ignoring the people who sought to detain him. "You doing all right?" he asked.

Cautiously she glanced around her and then back to him. "Your business associates are nuttier than squirrels," she said in a low voice.

He chuckled. "My sentiments exactly. Let's get out of here. We've got a full day tomorrow, with the press conference coming up."

During the taxi ride back, Jed pulled her to his side, pressing her head into his broad shoulder. "When do we leave?" she asked.

"The day after tomorrow. The production crew should be ready to start up at Ixtapa. Tired?"

"Very," she murmured, and snuggled against the hard, reassuring wall of his body. It had been a long, disconcerting day.

"And hungry, too, I'll bet. I'll have something sent up to the room."

Hungry? All she wanted to do was sleep. Her usual energy was gone. While Jed ordered up a light dinner, she stretched out on the color-splashed silk sofa that beckoned her and perused a guidebook provided by the hotel. Then, tired, she set the book back down. She meant only to close her eyes, to rest her bone-tired body, but it seemed mere minutes later that Jed was nudging her awake.

"Hey, Sleeping Beauty, dinner's served."

The tantalizing smell of food reached her senses first. Then Jed's touch. His lips dropped warm, petal-light kisses along her neck. She didn't move. Instead, eyes still closed, she let herself fully experience the heady sensation he aroused whenever he touched her. It was, she thought, a little like the county fair's Ferris wheel. Just the thought of going up and stopping and swinging, suspended so high above the earth, took her breath away, scared her. But she rode it anyway, because the funny somersaulting feeling she got in the pit of her stomach was like nothing else.

Blindly she turned her face toward his. His mouth lowered to hers, ruffling small kisses over her lips. Scorching hunger erupted in her body. She opened her mouth, wanting him inside her. At the touch of his tongue, at first slipping over her teeth in sweet, sensitive forays, then plunging inside, rapaciously claiming, she quivered uncontrollably. I'm like a mare, she thought, when the stud nips her flanks, and the shuddering ripple of muscles along her submissive body tells everything.

Now I know.

Jed's hands dropped to her shoulders, and his passion-dark eyes searched hers. She hid nothing, letting him see the love she had come to feel for him. He filled his palms with her small breasts, softly kneading, and beneath the silky material her nipples hardened in an ache that took her breath away and flushed her skin with heat.

He moved over her, still fully dressed. Instinctively she fitted herself to him, rejoicing in his hard strength. Her eyes relinquished his fierce, possessive stare and drifted dreamily closed as she felt, for the first time really felt, the mysterious responses of her body. Its secrets were unfolding; she was unfurling, like a sensuous, erotic bud ripe for flowering.

He crushed her lips with a demanding kiss, dragging her underlip into his mouth. Desperately seeking, his hand slid along her thigh, under her dress. At the warmth of his touch, her breath caught.

"Rob, honey," he whispered thickly, feverishly, "I have to stop now...or I won't stop at all."

An instinctive, ineluctable yearning within her wanted to discover this secret that was greater than the universe, this coming together that made two one. She wanted to have this to remember long after Jed had left Mescalero, when she was a leathery old spinster left with only dreams.

But even as her mouth opened to utter her assent, she recognized with astounding clarity that she was a coward. She didn't have her grandmother Ellie's courage, which had enabled the strong-willed pioneer woman to love two men, to take recklessly what her heart wanted and, afterward, willingly shoulder the consequences. Rob realized that the pain of watching Jed leave would be too much for her to bear. Instead of memories, she would have to make do with fantasies.

Jed must have seen her inner struggle. She watched him fight his own battle against desire...and win. He sat up and smoothed down her dress, which had ridden up to reveal the silky length of her thigh. His mouth twisted into a wry line. "I never was much for seducing reluctant maidens."

Chapter 12

Jed had lunch sent up, though he barely gave her time
to swallow her spinach quiche. He shot questions at
her, then prompted her if she was slow to answer.
"You're fresh meat for jaded journalists. They've
heard everything, Rob, and here's this young woman
right off the ranch. They'll be looking for your soft
spot, believe me—asking questions that violate your
privacy. You have to stay cool.

"Now, how do you feel about the acting profession?"

"I feel...it's given me an opportunity to see how the
other half lives."

"Good." He passed her a glass of wine. He was
walking, slowly circling the table, making it difficult
for her to think about eating.

Neither of them had mentioned the previous night. She hadn't slept well. At first she had tried to convince herself that it was sleeping in a different bed that kept her awake. But finally she had had to admit that it was her longing for Jed. Today the suite crackled with sensual electricity.

Now he was all business. "Did you fall in love with your leading man?"

She giggled, and he flashed her a stern look. "How could I fall in love with Tor?" she asked.

"You found him extremely attractive, but your heart belongs to Mescalero. Got it?"

She nodded, then took a swallow of the wine. It was sweet and pleasant-tasting.

"Not too much," he said, removing it from her reach. "You're not used to it. Now, let's say a reporter remarks on how you play the part of a wild and willful young woman who steals a restless man from his loving wife. Do you in any way in real life resemble that part?"

"Of course not!"

"You can't get defensive, Rob. Journalists are sharp—and skeptical. They may think the lady doth protest too much. Be gracious and charming and elusive. Say something like 'I'd love to think that I have such an extraordinary power, but after all, what I'm doing is only make-believe, isn't it?' You've turned the tables, see, putting them in the position of answering *your* question.

"Now—are you a virgin?"

Heat seared her skin. She caught his arched brow, his mocking glance, and forced a smile to her cold lips. "Only my doctor knows for sure."

Jed laughed. "I think you can handle the barracudas, sweetheart."

"I don't want to handle barracudas," she said, hearing the sadness in her voice. "Just horses."

He rubbed his beard-shadowed jaw. "If the film succeeds, Rob, you can have that cutting-horse ranch of yours and five more like it." He braced his hands on the table and said, "One more thing. Leave your hair loose."

She stared up at him. "What?" she whispered.

"Your hair. Leave it loose. You've constrained yourself long enough."

Six-thirty, and interview time had arrived. Dressed in the silk blouse and the rust-colored suede suit, she entered the conference room, with Jed protectively at her elbow. Flashes went off everywhere, momentarily blinding her. Jed led her to a lectern with a multitude of microphones. The sea of faces, the sudden babble of voices... her legs began to tremble. Then she felt Jed's touch at the small of her back, and he flashed her one of his reassuring winks, the way he always did just before she had to face the camera.

Then he stepped in front of her and gave the members of the media his full attention. "I'll lay down a few simple ground rules first," he told them, "and then I'll introduce you to the woman the whole world has been anxious to meet. Miss Malcolm's time is limited, so please keep your questions confined to *Sierra Sundown* and her role in it. Lastly, one question at a time, and please wait until you're given the floor."

Questions erupted immediately, and Jed called on a woman in the front row. Her question was innocuous enough, as were most of the others that followed. Then, from somewhere in the middle of the room, came the question "Are you in love with your director?"

Jed had coached her for something like this, but she hadn't expected the question to link her with Jed, or for it to stab her as deeply as it did. She managed a tight smile. "Aren't all women?"

"Miss Malcolm, the hotel has only Jed Pulaski registered," another voice said snidely. "Are you sleeping with him?"

She shut out the leering expressions, the jealous minds that would try to cheapen her love for Jed. Proud, untouchable, she stared calmly back at the predatory faces. They smelled blood.

Jed intervened, his smile gunmetal-hard. "I think you've just overstepped the boundaries of good—"

She touched his sleeve. "Please," she said quietly to him, "let me answer for myself."

She turned and faced the expectant reporters. "I don't have much education. Ranching—cattle and horses—that's about all I know. But this evening I learned that the term 'acted like animals' is an insult to the animal kingdom. Surely you've all heard of suites? Mr. Pulaski and I are sharing an extremely luxurious—and spacious—suite. We're no more sleeping together than those of you who live in apartments are sleeping with your next-door neighbor."

Some of the reporters shifted uncomfortably in their seats; others flinched. Jed took her elbow and cleared a path for her. Once they were outside the room, she pulled away.

"I need to get some fresh air, Jed. I feel smothered."

He captured her arm and tugged her toward the elevator. His expression was thunderous, but the harsh lines of his face softened when he saw her ashen face. "You should feel revolted by those bastards. Or maybe triumphant. Come on, you can get some fresh air out on our terrace."

"No, I need to go for a walk. By myself."

He pulled her inside the elevator and punched the top button. "Look, sweetheart. First, those pigs are going to dog your trail, and second, Mexico City at night isn't safe for a lone woman."

"You forget—I grew up surrounded by men. I can handle myself."

He backed her against the elevator wall, his forearms on either side of her head. She inhaled his warm, soap-clean scent. Maybe it was the rapidly rising elevator, or maybe it was the kisses he feathered over her face and hair, but funny things began to happen in her stomach. "I'm not forgetting anything," he growled, nuzzling her neck. "City men don't live by your cowboy code of honor."

His leg flexed between her thighs, bringing his body against hers, inch by inch. He used his mouth to rub her lips apart. She found it difficult to think logically. She was lost in the feverish hunger aroused by his kiss.

"Rob," he muttered, "I was so damned proud of you back there. I want you so badly, and it scares me to think that you might not want me."

The elevator door glided open, momentarily releasing her from his hypnotic power. He drew her along the entryway, but at the ringing of the telephone he halted, his mouth tightening impatiently. He released her long enough to cross to the sitting room and pick up the phone. "Yeah?" he barked into the receiver. Then, after a moment, he said, "She killed them, Maxwell. But you'll read all about it tomorrow. No, we leave tomorrow morning for Ixtapa, but I don't think..."

The sickening taste of the ugly interview returned. She spun away, seeking the breathing space for which her disheartened body clamored.

Jed hung up the receiver. With split-second clarity, and without even calling her name, he knew he was alone. Maybe that sixth sense developed by people like ranchers and miners was rubbing off on him. He simply knew that she was gone.

A cold, crushing feeling settled in his chest. He ran to the entryway. "Rob?"

He should have known better than to leave her alone, even for a moment. The ordeal this evening must have been traumatic for her.

He punched the elevator button, watching the floor numbers light up with agonizing slowness as it rose to the penthouse floor. It seemed just as slow in descending. In the lobby, guests, mostly Americans, milled around the registration desk. Others were standing in groups, conversing, or heading for the patio bar. He didn't spot her anywhere, but he recognized some of the members of the press from earlier this evening.

He was furious with them. Still, he should have realized that they would ferret out where Rob was staying. It had been foolish of him to install her in his suite, but he had wanted to keep her with him. And not just out of concern for her safety, but because he was selfish. She captivated him, made him feel an innocence he had never known.

He shoved his way through the crowd to the street. "Taxi, *señor*?" the doorman asked.

Jed shook his head. Calle Londres was jammed with evening strollers, sightseers, vendors. Where would she have gone? If she wandered too far in any direction, out of the Zona Rosa, she would be entering depressing neighborhoods where one more dead person in such a populous city would be nothing.

He started loping along the sidewalk, his heart pumping frantically. He pushed through a band of serenading mariachis, ignoring their blistering oaths.

Once he thought he spotted Rob. A tall woman with long, burnished brown hair was weaving in and out of the milling sightseers and window-shoppers. But when he grabbed the woman's shoulder and spun her around, she wasn't Rob. The woman began to shout what were no doubt Spanish obscenities. He left her still spouting vituperations and ran on.

Despair congealed his blood. Where would Rob have headed? At the brilliantly lighted intersection of Avenida Insurgentes and Avenida Chapultepec, boundaries of the Pink Zone, he was forced to wait for the roaring traffic to pass. The blinding automobile headlights and shrilling horns would be terrifying for someone like Rob, who had spent her life on a lonely ranch. He tried to imagine himself in her place. She'd done all he had requested with great aplomb, but now she must be soul-weary.

He stared impatiently at the stoplight; then his gaze alighted on the street sign. Chapultepec. Chapultepec Park! Just maybe! It wasn't that far from the Zona Rosa, a couple of miles at the most.

She would be heading not to romantic Montezuma's castle, sought out by tourists, but to the vast, seven-hundred-year-old zoo.

Despite his regular workouts on a boxer's speed bag, he was panting heavily by the time he reached the park. Maybe it was the altitude. Or too many cigarettes. Or—and the truth was painful—the fear of what might have happened to Rob.

At that time of night, the park was closed. Above it, the spotlighted castle majestically crowned Grasshopper Hill. He sprinted along the fence line. How would Rob have gained entry? Scaling the fence would be difficult, but not impossible. Still, with traffic streaming along the boulevard, a trespasser wouldn't go unobserved. Behind the railing, water from a moonlit lake reflected the park's lush botanical gardens. He loped on, past a stylized Indian fountain, then doubled back. The lava-rock troughs over which the water spilled formed an irregular staircase.

He removed his leather loafers and waded into the tiled pool. The rocks were slippery, and finding the right footholds was difficult. No doubt his escapade entertained passing motorists. When he reached the top, he realized that the back was a sheer wall. Well, it couldn't be any worse than reformatory walls. Holding on to the ledge, he let himself drop, grunting when he hit the soft earth.

Now where? If he were Rob, where would he head?

Suddenly he knew.

It took him almost a quarter of an hour to find the place. The mammoth trees filtered out the moonlight, so the flowered pathway encircling the pit was shrouded with shadows. When he couldn't find her, his heart lurched painfully. God, what if he'd been wrong? He'd been so damned sure. He should have called the police. Right now, somewhere else, she could be in danger...mugging...rape...his mind quickly closed off the ugly possibilities. By God, he'd find her first!

Something stirred in his peripheral vision, and he spun in that direction. His eyes focused on what turned out to be a stone bench—and Rob was sitting on it, her arms wrapped around her drawn-up legs, her chin resting on her knees.

Shoes dangling from one hand, he walked toward her. Her wet boots lay next to the bench. So she had entered the same way he had. When he stood beside her, she glanced up, her cheeks silvered with tear tracks.

"You're not surprised to see me?" he asked.

She shook her head. "Coming across the grass, you make more noise than a buffalo, Jed." She closed her eyes. "I'm learning that you don't let anything stand in the way of what you want, so I half expected you to track me down here." Her voice was raspy from crying.

His heart turned over at the sight of the pain he had brought on her. Years ago, he had made a decision never to consciously inflict pain on another human again. He hadn't boxed since, despite the pressure the navy and, later, two-bit promoters had placed on him. "Then you know I want you ... safe. With me."

She opened her eyes to focus on the animals that meandered around the pit, indifferent to their human observers. "How did you know where to find me?"

He managed a smile. He wanted to touch her, to hold her, but he tamped down the desire. "I figured that in this part of the city, zebras would be the closest to horses you could come.''

She closed her eyes. Bruised shadows lay beneath them. ''I feel like them, Jed. Like the zebras. All caged in, with no control over my life anymore.''

''I've been caged in, too, remember.''

Her eyes snapped open, and slowly she looked up at him. ''I've been waiting all this time for you to tell me about it.''

He circled around and slouched down beside her on the bench. He felt very weary. How had he let himself get mixed up with someone who didn't have any place in his life? Or he in hers? ''I killed a man, Rob.''

Surprise, but not condemnation, showed on her face. He was relieved. But she deserved to know the rest. ''You see, the man was my mother's boyfriend.''

He heard Rob's sharp intake of breath. Leaning forward, forearms on his thighs and shoes dangling between his knees, he said quietly, ''You see, my mother was a hopeless drug addict. She'd do anything to get what she needed, even sell herself. But it didn't matter what she was, or how abusive she could become, she was my mother, and I loved her.

''We didn't have any real home, just sleeping in condemned tenements, sometimes on the street, sometimes in charity places. Those were the best. A taste of heaven. But then you had to pay, because the do-gooders always insisted you confess your sins to save you from the hell they preached about. I had always figured hell was right there in the Hill District.

"Anyway, the day came when my mother had trouble even selling herself. The drugs had taken their toll. She looked fifty instead of thirty. I was twelve."

He paused, feeling sweat break out all over him, even though the night was cool. His lungs were doing double duty. "I awoke in the middle of the night when I heard screaming. She'd found some guy who didn't much care what she looked like, and after he'd gotten what he wanted, he started beating her. I started pummeling him and screaming and crying, trying to get him away from her. Then I touched something hard and cold. It was a gun, and I jerked it out of his jacket.

"Mother saw what I meant to do and tried to stop me. But she couldn't. I killed him. To wrap it up, after spending some time in a cell, I was sentenced to four years in reform school. As often as I ran away, I was always caught and returned. I still had a year to do when the navy offered to let me incorporate that final year into a four-year military-duty program. As it worked out, I was able to earn a liberal arts degree. A sort of fairy-tale ending, Rob, except that I have come to cherish my freedom more than anyone—*anyone*—can ever imagine."

Rob placed her hand on his arm, but she didn't say anything, didn't offer any platitudes, and for that he was grateful.

"So I can understand your feelings of being fenced in." He smiled ruefully and gave in to his urge to touch her moon-dappled hair. Its warmth didn't stave off the cold that had seeped into his heart. "I'll take you back to Mescalero tomorrow."

Her hair tangled around his fingers as she shook her head again. "No, I won't find peace there, either. Not yet. Not until we finish shooting here."

"Then come back to the hotel with me, Rob," he said, so softly that he couldn't hear his own voice for the singing of his blood in his veins.

Chapter 13

From the king-size bed, Rob watched Jed shrug out of his navy flannel blazer and tug loose his striped tie. His white shirt was open at the throat, revealing crisp golden-brown hair and tanned skin. His trousers, damp from the fountain, had been rolled up to his knees. Even with his muscular legs showing and in his bare feet, he looked so elegant, so at home among the rich trappings of the bedroom, that it was difficult to imagine him as the street kid who had fought his way through a tough neighborhood, reform school and the navy.

Tie dangling from one hand, he stood looking down at her for a moment, a long moment that made her blood race. "Stop worrying," she murmured. "I'm all right."

He turned and left her bedroom. She bit her lip to keep herself from calling out to him. Despite the bed's cozy warmth, despite the slip and silk blouse she still wore, she was shivering. She felt stripped of her security, of the self-awareness that had been her mainstay. She felt disoriented—and terribly lonely. She ached deep inside for something she couldn't identify, something she sensed she might never have.

From the other room came the clink of a bottle against glass; then he reappeared at the door, looping his tie over the knob. "I think you could use a drink," he said, extending the glass to her.

She eyed the amber liquid distrustfully, but took the drink. She almost flinched at the electrically charged contact with his fingers. How could he have so much sexual power over her?

"Go ahead, drink it," he said, sitting down beside her on the bed. His finely carved mouth stretched with a wry grin. "I promise it's not an aphrodisiac."

"Aphrodisiac?"

His smile betrayed his delight with her naiveté. "A stimulant—a love potion."

She felt the heat of a blush restore the warmth to her cheeks. "Things like that . . . aren't needed at Mescalero. The animals' urge to mate is strong."

"What about the humans?" he teased, but a passionate light was glinting in his eyes.

"Them too." Her breath felt choked, way down in her throat. "Me too."

Quietly he removed the glass from her chilled hands. His fingertip traced its rim, dipping inside to swirl the Scotch. She couldn't keep her gaze off his finger as it unhurriedly, sensuously stirred the amber liquor. Then he placed his finger, moist and scented with the heady aroma of the Scotch, on her lips. "Alcohol is sometimes used as a restorative," he said, his voice low, husky. "To bring someone back to their senses."

Her tongue touched his finger, tasted it. She heard the soft intake of his breath. "I don't need my senses restored," she said, catching his hand and bringing it to her cheek. "They're too—" she searched for the right word "—too sharp, too painful, as it is."

Ever so slowly, he bent toward her. She sensed him as a shadow, large and dark, blotting out the low light from the nightstand's lamp. "Where...where is it painful?" he asked softly.

"Here." She moved his hand to her heart. Beneath the silk of her blouse, her breast tightened at his touch.

He leaned over her, pushed her hair back from her neck and kissed her there. Like a mare being mounted, she submitted docilely to his gentle nipping. Ripple upon ripple of pure pleasure eddied over her, and she quivered violently. "Yes," she gasped. "Yes, Jed."

"You want this?" he whispered fiercely.

"I...yes, I want this."

He never took his eyes off her face as he rose and stripped off his shirt and trousers. Enraptured, she gazed at the broad expanse of his chest, his flat stomach and the strong shape of his legs. A fiery yearning swept through her.

Drawing back the satin coverlet, he lay down beside her, pulling her into the curve of his arm. His hard length ... There was so much more strength in him than in her. His flesh was rough, matted with hair. She moved against him, wanting to feel him atop her. Against her stomach she felt the ridge of his flesh expanding, hardening. So this was what it meant to be a woman, to take pleasure in a man. Her man.

He began to unfasten her blouse. He must have done this many times, but it pleased her to note that his hands trembled with his need of her. Cool air rushed over her exposed breasts, and then he began to stroke her nipples through the lacy fabric of her bra. Her eyes closed, and she moaned and strained against him.

"There's no rush, sweetheart. Instant gratification is fleeting." He lowered his mouth over one nipple, and his tongue explored it with unhurried delight. She stared at his tawny head while all sorts of exquisite sensations zephyred through her. Then the sensations became too much. Her head lolled back on the pillow, and she made little mewling sounds that she would never have associated with herself. When his teeth gently released the tight bud, the air wafted in to nip erotically at taut flesh that wasn't quite dry.

She sighed as his lips, firm, warm, grazed the quivering corners of her mouth. His earthy male smell filled her nostrils, and she could feel herself losing control. Her legs spread in welcome for his hand. It paused, resting on the nylon-clad mound of her femininity. His clear amber eyes studied her with tenderness. "I've never placed any particular importance on that thin tissue that makes a woman a virgin. But I need to know if you do."

"I never thought about it," she answered honestly. "I never thought about wanting...this."

He drew off her panties and touched her again... there, where she felt all moist. There, where she had so long been neglected. "You're hot and love-ready."

She knew he was giving her a final opportunity to change her mind. "Yes. I have been for a long time now, Jed. I want you inside me."

His finger slid inside her protective folds, deep inside, and began to move in rhythmic motions. She gasped and moaned aloud. Her hands knotted the sheet, and he pried her fingers loose. "Feel what you do to me," he said, drawing her hand down to rest over his heart. The rapid pounding was almost frightening to her.

Something in her face, the rapture that engulfed her as he continued his sensuous torment, must have ignited an answering fire in him, because he pushed her hands above her head, pinning them there, and levered himself atop her. He was heavy, so heavy, so good.

"It should have been someone else for you, Rob," he muttered. "Someone else...another rancher... showing you how to love. Not me."

"No, only you." Because no matter how different they were, how mismatched, there was still some primal connection between them. She was sure this didn't happen to everyone. Certainly she had never expected it to happen to her.

"Oh, dear God," he murmured against her throat. "We're both lost."

Then, as if surrendering to a relentless desire, he released her wrists and slid his hands under her thighs, cupping her hips as he entered her, filling her. There was no sharp pain, only the initial discomfort of adjusting herself to him. She whimpered, and he planted feverish kisses all over her face. "So sweet, so good, my little wild creature."

She clutched his shoulders and marveled at the strength of his muscles, the expansion and contraction of his rib cage with each great gasp he uttered. She trailed little kisses over one shoulder, finding that he tasted salty and masculine. Her fingers strayed elsewhere, caressing him and delighting in feeling him tighten under her touch. She stared up into his dark, impassioned face. He looked younger, less cynical. Her hand slipped up his neck, its muscles strained and taut, then moved farther up to touch one cheekbone. "I might have missed all this," she whispered wonderingly. "The loving."

He went rigid and rolled away, staring down at her, studying each feature of her face. Then, as if satisfied, he fitted his mouth onto hers with a low groan, kissing her gently, deeply. "Kiss me back, Rob."

She angled her head and ran the tip of her tongue over the puckered scar that adorned his lip. His breath hissed in. "Are there other scars I can kiss?" she asked, smiling more at her own audacity than at the growing sensual pleasure she saw in his taut expression.

"Yeah," he growled. "An appendix scar."

She didn't remember seeing one. Her eyes narrowed, and she said, "Let me feel."

Leaning to one side, he took her hand and guided it down over his rib cage to his flat stomach and the wiry curls clustered there. Suddenly the cylindrical flesh burned her fingertips. "That's not a . . ."

Her words trailed off as she felt his sex rapidly swell. Her fingers closed around the velvet heat, their sensitive tips tracing his throbbing length. He groaned and caught her wrist. "Enough—or there won't be enough."

She smiled a womanly smile, and began to rock him, her hand soothing and stroking, her eager mouth raining kisses on his mouth, his eyes, his hair. Without intending to, she began to chant love words. She wanted him more in that moment than she would ever have believed it possible for her to want someone.

He moved over her, taking command. He slid into her with infinite slowness, his thickness stretching her, filling her. He began to stroke the length and breadth of her, painting golden sunlight inside her. She understood now what she was made for. Her fingers dug into his shoulders, their muscles strained and enormous. Then his body took over, plunging into her with increasing intensity until he was pounding her with a passionate fury. Silky fire flowed into her like crimson waves. She bucked back, riding with him on this white-hot journey of rapture.

"Come on," he urged against her parted lips. "Let go. Let yourself go!"

She did as he told her—not that she had any choice—and an explosive, incredibly pleasurable sensation overtook her. Tiny fires burst inside her, convulsing her muscles. He held her fast, but she arched into him, and when her hips once more began their sinuous motion, he quickly withdrew. His mouth drew back in what might have been a snarl, and he shuddered with the effort it took to bring himself back under control.

For a moment he lay there, gasping, and she clasped his head against the hollow of her neck. His lips grazed the throbbing pulse there, and he said, "I'm sorry, Rob. If it had to happen, I'm sorry it had to be like this."

She tilted her head so that she could look down at his profile. A mellow feeling, a sense of utter peace such as she had never known, spread over her. She understood now this fierce drive to mate. "I would have kept you inside me. I would have had all of you."

"But the last thing you need is to get..." He trailed off, running a practiced hand down her rib cage. "Tomorrow you're going to be terribly tender here," he said, touching her between her thighs and tracing circles in the damp cleft.

A shock of desire shot through her, and her body bucked at the high sensual voltage. Impossible, from just his touch!

He uncoiled himself from the bed and strode into the bathroom, then returned with a warm, damp washcloth. Her gaze hungered after his beautiful body...supple, toasted, hard...and his rigid, straining flesh. How horrible it would have been, she mused, if she had fallen in love with a man who was embarrassed by his body, or found sex distasteful.

Almost tenderly, Jed wiped the moisture of their loving from her belly and thighs. "You're astonishingly beautiful underneath all that masculine clothing you usually wear," he told her, his eyes following the path of the washcloth. "I find myself very glad that you hid that beauty for so long."

Watching him, she realized how much she loved him. She could never go back to being the incomplete woman she had been before. She put her hand on his. He paused, glancing up at her questioningly. "When I was just a kid, Jed, I remember Tom reading me the story about the ugly duckling that turned into a swan. For a long time after I was sad, because I knew I'd always be an ugly duckling."

A small, thoughtful frown deepened the lines that fanned out around his eyes. "I wonder if any of us ever get over childhood. When I was in reform school, I'd wake up scared and breathing hard from a terrible dream of loneliness, of the horror of what I'd done. When I grew up, I learned that that fear never goes away. You have to live with it, as you have to live with all your memories and all your experiences."

She could sense him withdrawing from her. "Jed?"

"Mmm?"

"Would you kiss me?"

He raised himself on one elbow and gingerly pushed the tumbled hair from her face to study it seriously. "I don't think there's anyone quite like you, Rob." Then he bent over her and placed a light but lingering kiss on her lips.

She inhaled his warm breath. He was so strong and beautiful. She wanted to memorize everything about him for those moments when she wasn't with him. She pulled away, her head tilted, to eye him speculatively. "Are men like horses?"

"What?"

"Well, I mean, do men have to wait a long time before . . . uh, before they can mount again?"

He erupted in laughter and gathered her against him. "Oh, Rob, sweetheart, I enjoy you so damn much! Too damn much!" Then his laughter turned to hungry little kisses as his mouth began to move ravishingly over her body.

* * *

Jed woke her the next morning with light, breathy kisses that tasted faintly of coffee and toothpaste and himself. "I thought you ranch women got up with the rooster's first crow," he said teasingly.

She stretched lazily, a sleepy grin curving her dusky lips. "I never felt so good. All over."

"There's coffee and croissants on the nightstand," he said, heading for the bathroom. "Drink up, because we've got a flight to catch this morning."

She watched him through the open bathroom door. He shaved naked, and she couldn't help but think how gorgeous a man's body was. He stretched his mouth to one side, smoothing a path for his razor and bypassing the scar riding his upper lip. Then he bent over the sink to get a better view of his foam-smeared jaw, causing the muscles in his back to shift.

Her gaze drifted downward to his tight, rounded buttocks and the solid length of his legs. Was she becoming obsessed with Jed, as Tom had become obsessed with Marianna when she first came to Mescalero?

Rob wondered why she had never given any thought to men and the wonder of sex. Because she had thought she was too independent to need a man? How the other women must have laughed at her!

Hands braced on the sink, Jed was staring at her in the mirror. His eyes were heated with sensual longing. From the look of him, he was obviously aroused again.

How would she ever be able to go back to Mescalero, to a life-style that hadn't changed in centuries, inside a body that had changed overnight? She would never be the same again, and in a way she was worse off—because now she knew what had been missing from her life.

Sliding the sheet off her, she got out of bed, then padded naked across the carpet and came up behind him. She pressed herself against him, feeling the hard muscles of his hips.

In the mirror, his eyes squinched closed and his mouth contorted. He lowered his head, and his hands gripped the counter's edge. "Rob...don't let yourself get too involved."

Her heart was racing. "I can hold my own."

Chapter 14

Okay, first team back in," Jed shouted above the
roar of the Pacific breakers pounding the beach.

Reluctantly Rob stepped out from the shade of a
coconut palm. The fierce heat, intensified by the sun
reflecting off the ocean, didn't bother her. It was the
wet air. Having been raised in the desert's dry cli-
mate, she wasn't accustomed to breathing air so thick
with moisture that oxygen was at a premium. Perspiration poured off her, and her skin felt sticky, dirty. Of
course, it was supposed to look that way anyway for
the upcoming scenes.

From what Jed had explained to her, the Mexican
scenes covered the Gypsy girl's life in a camp that dealt
in horse-trading and ended with her fleeing an arranged wedding during a Pacific squall. But it was

taking all morning just to shoot one short encounter. One of the camera generators wasn't working, and by the time another was brought in, clouds had massed, so Jed had to halt production until they dissipated.

In this particular scene, the Gypsies were offering their wares in a fishing town. "Okay," Jack, the assistant director, said, "all you background folks move up to the center of the screen."

The extras took their places on the cobblestone street fronting Zihuatanejo's bay. One extra was to play the guitar, another the flute. One man, a scarf tied around his head, would do acrobatics for the Mexican peasants. Women, dressed in the Gypsys' traditional swirling skirts and heavy jewelry, would tell fortunes, drive the colorful carts and sell good-luck medals.

Rob took her position on the tailgate of a brilliant red cart. A strange wagon full of dreams, she thought, and her gaze automatically sought out Jed. He was instructing a dark, rotund man on how he was to play the scene as the Gypsy king, her uncle. Jed looked hard and implacable. He was a man who wouldn't be fooled. Recalling his smoldering eyes, his warm breath tickling the shell of her ear, she shivered with a different kind of heat. It was incredible, the way she was attracted to this powerful, commanding man, when, for as long as she could remember, she'd rebelled against male domination. Crazy, the feelings of desire he was able to arouse in her.

All her life she had worked hard for her dream of a place of her own, a cutting-horse ranch, and now, in a few short months, he had vanquished her dream, replacing it with himself. She shouldn't have let this happen to her. Shouldn't have let herself love him. He had never mentioned love. Once he returned to his Hollywood life, she would have nothing.... Her dream no longer mattered, and he, too, would be gone.

Marcie came over and dabbed the perspiration from Rob's face, and then it was time to shoot.

"Roll, please," Jed called.

"Rolling!" Linda responded.

"Rock the wagon," Jed told two men off camera. "Let's have the dust!"

The wagon began to rock. A woman off camera spewed baby powder from a pressurized paint sprayer. Rob tried not to sneeze.

"Look tired," Jed instructed her.

That wasn't difficult. She felt exhausted.

"That's it, honey," he said encouragingly, but a moment later he called, "Cut!"

He came over and, hands at her waist, lifted her down from the tailgate. His amber gaze searched her face. "Are you all right?"

"It's the air," she murmured. *And you.* "There's not enough of it." *Whenever you come near me, touch me, I can't breathe right.*

"The humidity saps your strength. Come on, let's get you back to the hotel. We'll pick this up later, people," he called, then led her away.

He hailed a waiting Volkswagen, one of the many local taxis hired for the duration of the shoot, and ushered her inside. Her legs were too long for the compact car, and she ended up wedged against Jed, feeding fire right back into her blood. As the little taxi sped along the single-lane road, which wound over a ridge, the lowered windows sucked in the steamy air. They were too hot to talk. She was content to be held in the circle of his arm, her head resting on his shoulder.

She never used to get tired—if anything, she had had too much energy—but these days... How had Marianna managed to maintain the hectic pace of filming without becoming drained? How had she exposed her private feelings for everyone to see? Rob could only admire her sister-in-law that much more.

They made the five-mile trip from the fishing village of Zihuatanejo to the government-built resort of Ixtapa in grand-prix time. Because of its location, Ixtapa was less overgrown with vegetation than the neighboring village, and much cooler. Its pristine white bay captured the sea breeze, so the air-conditioning in the prestigious hotels was almost superfluous.

When they arrived at their hotel, Rob noticed anxiously that the Saltillo-tiled lobby was as busy as a box full of kittens, full of arriving and departing guests, who stared at her outlandish costume. Though she still wasn't accustomed to being a source of curiosity, she carried herself with such confidence that no one suspected she was ill at ease. And with the veneer of sophistication that she had acquired from Jed, she appeared to be the woman all other women longed to emulate.

The glass elevator took her away from the inquisitive stares, conveying the two of them up to an airy and elegant suite that overlooked the sparkling turquoise ocean. She immediately headed for the private terrace, completely screened from the view of others, pushing aside the plate-glass door and bypassing the white wicker patio furniture and turning her face toward the Pacific.

Never having seen an ocean before, she couldn't get enough of watching it. The feel of the salty breeze on her skin, the vast expanse of the sea...in a way, she might have been back at Mescalero. The desert breeze was drier, and its vast expanse was sand, not water, but all she needed was its vastness...and to love Jed.

He put his hands on her shoulders and turned her to face him. The gold in his eyes had darkened and turned molten. "Where have your thoughts taken you?"

She hesitated, wishing she had it in her to be anything but forthright. "Mescalero."

She watched him carefully school his expression into blandness. "I should have guessed."

"Someday...one day, I'd like to show you my place, Slaughter Mesa. The Apaches committed bloodcurdling murders there, and the place has the grisly reputation of being haunted by their victims. Another legend says it's haunted by a love that was never fulfilled, my grandma Ellie's. But I feel only a great peacefulness there."

There was something in his eyes.... "Rob, the day after tomorrow, I have to fly up to L.A.—to get the ball rolling on postproduction. We're running behind as it is. Jack will take over shooting the remaining scenes here and at Mescalero until I can get back. I'll try to hurry. I shouldn't be gone more than two or three weeks at the most."

Her throat felt as if she had eaten a particularly hot chili pepper, and her eyes burned, but she didn't say anything. She couldn't.

"Rob, it would never work." His grip bruised her shoulders. "You'd be miserable traveling around the globe with me. Always the unfamiliar. Missing your family—old Red Eye, Tom, Rand, Colt and the rest. And I'd be miserable confined by Mescalero's isolation, Rob." He almost shook her. "Don't you see? We would only destroy each other!"

She stared back at the features that haunted her dreams. "You don't believe that love—deep, real love—overcomes all obstacles?" she asked in quiet desperation. "What about Sir Walter Scott, and Shakespeare?"

His eyes were bleak. "Fiction. Fairy tales." He pushed an errant lock of her unbound hair behind one ear and looked at her solemnly. "Remember, I deal in distortion, sweetheart."

Distractedly he ran his fingers through his hair, and she caught his hand. "Jed, I'm brave enough to risk it. Why aren't you?"

"You and your Old West values and virtues. You think your shining belief in black and white, in good and bad, will fix everything, don't you?" he whispered, ruffling her wild curls.

He rubbed his knuckles against her lips, and she inhaled deeply of his smell, shuddering all the way through to her core. "Yes. Yes!"

There was a long, silent pause. The air was thick with waiting. Then he cupped the back of her neck and drew her face to his. "Maybe, just maybe, it could," he muttered against her trembling lips.

He kissed her with feverish urgency. His hands moved passionately over her shoulders and her breasts, cupped her hips, closing her in against the hard mound at the apex of his legs. Her fingers tore hastily at his shirt, his belt buckle. There was only this moment, because she didn't trust the future.

He pushed down her off-the-shoulder blouse. Her creamy, rose-tipped breasts swung free, and he made a low, involuntary rasping sound. The sea breeze playing over her naked skin hardened her nipples to little brown raisins.

"Oh, Rob," he murmured. "Lovely...untouched."

She couldn't catch everything he was saying, but his blunt fingers plucked and rotated one turgid nipple, making her gasp. "Kiss me there!" she begged.

He dipped his head, taking the aching nipple into his mouth. She held his head pressed to her soft breast, feeling the blood surge to the engorged tip. Her knees buckled with the exquisite pleasure. He picked her up and lowered her onto the chaise longue's lime-colored cushion. The sun-heated vinyl scorched her bare shoulders and thighs where he had shoved her skirt above her hips.

He stripped off his belt and dropped it on the wicker table. "I need to get deep inside you, Rob, to feel how sweet you are, to feel you tight and hot around me."

He unzipped his khaki trousers to reveal his swollen flesh jutting against his black briefs. Without even fully removing his clothes, he knelt over her and entered her. A silky fire burned its way through her, smoldering and sparking. With a small cry, she sought out his mouth. His tongue teased her lips and teeth, then entered and withdrew from her mouth in tempo with his fierce, driving rhythm as he sheathed himself inside her.

"Un coup de foudre!" The words were a rush of breath against her ear.

Delicious goose bumps mottled her skin. "I've never heard that phrase," she said, nipping his earlobe. "It doesn't even sound like Spanish."

"French . . . Rob." He timed his words with each deep stroke he delivered. "For. . . a thunderbolt. From the moment I watched . . . you at the dinner table . . . I began acting as if I'd been struck . . . by lightning."

She smiled, but then he began to withdraw, and she was afraid it would be like before, leaving her empty. Then he filled her with himself in a different way. He slipped down the length of the chaise until his hands found her ankles and spread them on either side of the cushioned seat. She gasped when he plunged his head between her spread thighs. This was something about which she was entirely ignorant. Nothing could have prepared her for this. She shoved at his shoulders, but the hard, hot tongue flicking against her moist cleft sent shock after shock through her, electrifying her flesh.

Her fingernails dug half-moons into his shoulders, and her head lolled to one side, her breath coming in short, jerky gasps. Her lids, heavy with languor, fluttered closed. Her body began to twitch convulsively, and the faint whimpering noises coming from her lips evolved into a cry of intense, crescendoing pleasure.

For long, shuddering moments, she lay still. Gradually the sea breeze revived her—that and Jed's tender kisses over her bare shoulder. He had slid up beside her, lying half atop her, so masculinely heavy. Now he gathered her against him, and she could feel his leashed power.

This was the kind of man she needed, she thought. A man who could hold his own with her. Images of him flitted across the back of her lids . . . him hunkered over the pool table; him teaching her how to dance; the afternoon in the tack room, when he had tenderly ministered to the lacerations on her back; his tormented expression at the cockfight; and, later, his sharing his breath with her, bonding her to him.

Yes, he had done that . . . bonded her to him forever.

Dreamily she opened her eyes and twined her arms tightly around his neck. His face was strained with his unspent need. "Jed, this isn't fair," she said in a breathless whisper. "What about you?"

He nipped her earlobe. "Take me in hand," he said, his voice husky. "Do the same to me."

Her hands began to trace the taut lines of his powerful body. He shifted, exposing himself to her to do with as she liked. Wherever she touched him, his muscles jumped convulsively, and a grating sound erupted from his compressed lips as she stroked him. His fingers clenched and unclenched in her hair. She marveled at the bursting strength of him. Aroused again herself, she increased her pressure, her tempo, until he overflowed.

Tenderly she gazed down at his hard, rugged face, his closed eyes, the dark sweep of his lashes. "I love you," she whispered.

"Oh, Rob," he muttered thickly into her shoulder. "What are we going to do?"

"Roll out the wind machine," Jed instructed one of the key grips.

The cast and extras were clustered in a meadow that was bounded on one side by ocean cliffs and on the other by a coconut plantation. The cameras had been set up at an angle to capture both vistas without including the plantation's nearby hacienda and accompanying utility poles.

The machine was rolled out of one of the semis and down a ramp. "Rehearsals," Jed said. "And background. Quiet, please."

Rob took her place in the circle of Gypsies and caravans. Her heart began to knock ridiculously against her rib cage as Jed came over to her. He looked tired. She knew he hadn't slept well the night before. She had awakened to find him out on the terrace, smoking, watching the breakers smash against the beach. She had said nothing to disturb his private thoughts. For that hour, her loving gaze had adored his glorious, naked body; then, when he returned to bed, she had feigned sleep.

"Now, look, Rob, as the violins begin to play and the wedding is about to start, the camera pans to you. Your face has got to say it all . . . your discontent with your prospective groom, your wanderlust and, at the same time, your fear of flouting Gypsy tradition."

She nodded. The sun was a semicircle of red on the edge of the Pacific, but in the tropical heat, sweat was still beaded all over her, although she would have been perspiring had the scene been filmed in the Arctic. It was bad enough revealing her emotions before everyone, but just the thought of filming without Jed there to serve as a sort of an invisible wall between her and the others almost paralyzed her with fear.

The rehearsal went all right, but she went through seventeen takes of the rollicking wedding feast—Gypsy men in baggy pants madly sawing away on fiddles, the women wildly dancing.

"Roll sound," Jed said, and the "Gypsies" began singing.

"I'm not from these parts,
I wasn't born near.
The wheel of fortune, spinning, spinning,
Has brought me here."

"That's a take," Jed said at last.

The scene in which Rob stood with her intended before the Gypsy king for the wedding ceremony went no better. When the storm was supposed to arise and she was to flee the ceremony, the wind machine wouldn't work. Finally the electricians got it going, but on the first take, the tremendous wind blew her skirts up over her head for a most improper shot. Subsequent takes went no better.

"Take 7," Jed grunted, and that time they finally got it right.

Then came the shot of her fleeing the Gypsy camp. She was to run blindly among the palm trees while the wind machine blew with hurricane force. A few enraged Gypsies were to follow her, plunging through the lush undergrowth and firing their pistols at her. For this, certain trees, as well as herself, had to be prepped by the special-effects people, loaded with wads of powder and wired with detonators.

While Jed blocked out the scene for her five Gypsy pursuers, she surrendered herself to the special-effects group. She noticed that Charlie jockeyed with the others for the opportunity to wire her for the pistol shot that was to wound her. His hand slipped suggestively over her skin, and she kept her glance averted, bothered by the forced intimacy.

"Looks like the shrew has been tamed."

Her gaze moved from the green hillside to his impudent grin. "I beg your pardon?"

"Yeah, baby, you know. Ever heard of Shakespeare?"

She turned to face him fully. "Do you want to tell me what you're talking about?"

"I don't guess you have."

"I'm not the village idiot. I know who Shakespeare was!"

He glanced nervously over to where Jed was conversing with the five extras. "Well...it was no secret that Pulaski told Peter Maxwell that he'd tame you."

Charlie's cocky grin faded, and his glance slid apprehensively to her furious expression. "Look, it's none of my business. Everyone just assumed that since Pulaski and you have been pretty close lately and he's taking off for L.A. tomorrow...well... Look, I'm sorry if I spilled the beans and all. I just thought..." His words trailed off as he sheepishly backed away from her stony countenance.

* * *

"Rob!"

She halted. The roar of the powerful waves crashing against the shore was deafening, and the wind was whistling against her ear, reminding her of the time when she had once held a seashell to it. Yet she knew that she had heard Jed call her name. Slowly she turned to watch him run along the moonlit beach toward her. Getting through the rest of the filming that day had been torture. Facing him now would be hell.

He caught up with her and grabbed her shoulders. "Where have you been? I've looked everywhere! Why didn't you wait to ride back with me?" He was practically shaking her.

She shrugged. "I needed a walk."

"You could have walked to Puerto Vallarta and back by now," he snarled. "Do you have any idea what time it is?"

Indifferently she glanced up at the moon. "A little bit past midnight, I imagine."

He groaned and hugged her against him. "Rob, what is it? Is it Mescalero you're missing?"

The quiet rage that had been building in her ripped free. She pulled herself out of his embrace. "I trusted you!"

His brows lowered in a puzzled frown. "What?"

"Taming the shrew!" she cried. "Charley told me all about what you told Maxwell—how you planned to break me like some wild horse!"

He dug his fingers through his wind-whipped hair. Anguish darkened his face. "I did—but, dear God, Rob, how was I to know I'd fall in love with you?"

She should have been appeased by his confession of love, but her powerful Malcolm pride, her woman's pride, had been wounded. For the first time she fought back as a woman. "You don't know black from white, do you? It's all gray in your world, Jed! Well, I hate your world, do you hear me?"

She spun away, but he caught her wrist and jerked her back to him. His face was thunderous. "You don't know anything about my world! How dare you judge me?"

She shoved desperately at him, staggering him, and spun away, only to lose her own balance and stumble to her knees. Jed latched on to her ankle, halting her before she could scramble away. She twisted onto her back and kicked out, but he fell on top of her, crushing the breath from her lungs.

"Get off me!" she screamed. "You used me!" She bit his neck, tasting the salty flesh.

He twisted free and slanted his mouth roughly over hers. She compressed her lips, but his tongue jammed them apart. "Go ahead, bite me!" he ordered. "Taste my blood. It runs as thick and proud as yours. And as hot!"

She *was* hot. As frenzied as a mare in mating season. She wanted him, and her tongue dueled with his as she bucked against him in liquid, mindless shivers.

"Oh, yes, sweetheart." His rough excitement matched her wild abandon. Her hands clumsily fumbled with his zipper. The sand abraded her hips as he yanked down her panties. When he invaded her with his sure mastery, she clutched his shoulders, feeling the powerful muscles contract. Stroke after stroke, he moved into and out of her, riding her madly, making her his all over again. With a triumphant cry, he poured himself into her at last.

For long, panting moments, they lay there on the sand until the creeping tide nudged their feet. He raised himself up on his elbows then and stared tenderly down at her. His thumb glided over her kiss-swollen lips and grazed the satiny skin just inside. "Rob, I love you."

She stared defiantly up at him. A sad smile curved his mouth, and his eyes were luminous, catching the light reflected off the water. "Rob, listen to me. The beauty in loving someone is in the relationship, in the struggle. It's people doing their best, slipping and falling and helping each other back up. The richness of love lies in its complexity. Will you forgive me?"

Tears seeped from the corners of her eyes. "Oh, Jed, what's to become of us?"

"I don't know, but I've been giving it a lot of thought. We could buy a place in the San Fernando Valley, maybe. Build a horse ranch." Gingerly, as if holding a fragile desert flower, he took her face in his big hands. "We might just make it work, sweetheart."

She wanted to believe that. Wanted to believe that, whatever it took, she could do it, whatever compromises were needed, she could make them. She had been raised to face hardships. Now she would merely be exchanging one kind for another.

Chapter 15

Landis stepped down from the van parked in the Mescalero yard and carelessly passed her carryon to Emmitt. Her gaze was trained on Rob Malcolm, who was feeding an apple to one of her horses in the nearest corral. The young woman wore hip-hugging jeans and a raspberry cotton blouse that had a tailored, designer-label look. There was a certain dignity, a certain aura, about her that hadn't been there at the beginning of the filming. Landis was sure of that.

And she was just as sure that she now stood a good chance of losing her bid for an Oscar, knocked out of the running by this dark horse. How appropriate, she thought ironically.

* * *

When it came to being a woman, Rob still felt in-adequate. She had so much to learn, and the process was painfully difficult.

A dozen times since her arrival the day before she had been tempted to call Jed in California. From what he had told her before he'd left, he was terribly busy—rushing, in fact, just so that he could get back to Mescalero ahead of schedule.

"Anything wrong, Rob?"

Almost shyly, she glanced over at Haydee, who was slicing a frozen square of herbed butter onto each of fifteen chicken breasts laid out on waxed paper. Since shooting didn't resume until tomorrow, Rob had of-fered to pitch in and help with the evening meal, and at the moment the two of them were alone in the kitchen.

Rob looked up from the tomatoes she was dicing. She was helpless in the kitchen when it came to actual cooking. She hadn't been bred for domesticity. What would happen when Jed wanted to entertain? "Hay-dee . . . you lived in California. Would I like it there?"

"I suppose so." Haydee slanted Rob a curious look. "My life there was pretty wrapped up in the univer-sity. Why don't you ask Marianna? She would be able to tell you better than I can."

"Maybe I will." But she wouldn't. Marianna was different. Marianna had an inner strength. She was one of those special people—the beautiful and the rich and the famous—set apart from the rest of the world's mere mortals. Marianna could adapt anywhere.

"So, you've got your sights set on Jed Pulaski?" Haydee asked.

Rob swallowed. "Has everyone been talking?"

"Not that I know of. It just seemed to me that he was the only man that might be able to work well in harness with you."

Rob had to smile, even though tears scratched the back of her throat. "You're starting to talk like a ranch hand, Haydee." She concentrated on dumping the tomatoes into a large stainless-steel bowl and said, "I love Jed. More than I thought it was possible for me ever to love anyone. But Jed and me, we're different breeds."

"Look, Rob, a real woman—if she wants a man—goes after him. The way I'm going after your nephew."

Rob flicked her a look of astonishment. "Rand? But you won't even give him the time of day!"

Haydee grinned mischievously. "Exactly. Just what I was trying to tell you. You do whatever it takes."

Rob kept Haydee's advice in mind as she hurriedly changed for dinner. The old Rob would have been content with washing her hands and face. The new Rob took a quick shower, laved baby oil over every inch of her skin and touched perfume behind her ears and at her throat and wrists. Then she slipped into a crimson knit dress that clung dramatically to her subtle curves. With her black heels, she was over six feet. She smiled back at the incredibly beautiful, exotic young woman reflected in the antique cheval mirror. She still had a hard time believing this was her.

Jed wasn't due in tonight—not for at least another week, in fact—but she had learned something about looking one's best as often as possible. It was not only pleasant for others, it said something about one's respect for oneself.

When she reached the dining room, members of the cast and crew were still straggling in. Charley, she noted, wasn't among them.

The Malcolms were all there, though. With affection, she glanced around at the familiar faces. Old Red Eye, whose rheumy eyes revealed too much imbibing the night before; Colt, too silent and too caring; Rand, with his infectious smile; Shyloh, whose velvety doe eyes conflicted with her unruly buffalo's mane.

Then there were Tom and Marianna. Her brother had been everything to her until Jed had intruded into her life. Tom and Marianna offered her hope that sometimes love did triumph. It didn't have to go unrequited, as had Grandma Ellie's love for Red Eye. The love between Tom and Marianna demonstrated that happiness was possible, even between two wildly mismatched people.

"It's been right quiet here without you, Rob," Rand said, passing a platter of scalloped potatoes.

"Admit it, you missed me," she teased.

The expressions on the faces of the other Malcolms were evidence of their astonishment. She glanced from one to the next. "Did I say something wrong?"

Tom shrugged. "We're just not used to you teasing, darlin'." His shrewd eyes flickered over her dress. "You look mighty pretty tonight."

She blushed violently. "Thought I'd try something different for a change."

In the ensuing silence, Rand came to her rescue, saying laconically, "It's been so dry while you were gone, Rob, that it would take forty acres to rust a nail."

With the chuckle that went around the table, her tension eased, and the rest of the meal passed pleasantly.

The urge to call Jed was strongest in the middle of the night, the loneliest time of all. She hadn't known loneliness until he had appeared on the scene to take charge of her life. She wasn't sleeping at all these days, and it showed in the shadows beneath her eyes. Marcie had noticed them and insisted on applying a highlighter under Rob's makeup.

Eight days had passed since her return to Mescalero, and she hadn't heard from Jed. It was almost three weeks since she had seen him! He might be busy during the day, but surely, come nightfall . . . No, Jed didn't equate night with rest. He ran on pure adrenaline.

She really wanted to believe he was working furiously in order to get back to Mescalero that much sooner, but she had heard tales of the Hollywood high life, and she couldn't help but worry.

With lethargic steps, she headed toward the barn and Death Threat. Today she would be riding the beast for the first time in more than four weeks. She had gotten only a couple of yards from the veranda when Marianna stuck her head out the door and called, "Telephone, Rob."

At the smile on her sister-in-law's face, Rob's heart lurched with wild hope. Her hand shaking, she picked up the hall telephone. "Yes?"

"Rob." The long-distance static on the line roughened Jed's smooth baritone voice, but the sound of it still did funny things to her, left her weak all over and made her pulse pound in her ears. "I miss you."

"Jed," she said softly, "I didn't know what lonely was until you left!" There was so much that she wanted to ask ... whether he still loved her ... but she didn't know who might overhear the conversation. And her feelings for Jed were very private, very personal. "When are you coming back?"

"Soon. I've got a boatload of problems to sort out here, but I'm catching the first horse back. I promise."

His attempt at lightheartedness sounded flat. She suspected he was exhausted. Or was he just avoiding making a commitment? Was she fooling herself? No, she had to trust him.

"Behave yourself, sweetheart, and don't give Jack and Maxwell any problems. You're a handful, even when you're on your best behavior. Gotta go now. Hey, Rob...don't forget me."

How could she?

Reluctantly she relinquished the telephone and set out once more for the barn. Usually the challenge of mastering a rogue horse sent her own adrenaline surging, but at that moment she felt only a heavy sadness—and, she supposed, a certain relief that she would only have to ride the berserk animal for a few more scenes.

Today's scene wasn't scheduled until late in the afternoon, but she knew she had better establish some kind of rapport with the animal.

Death Threat greeted her with a wild neighing and the furious stamping of his hooves. "Well, welcome to the mutual abomination society," she told him glumly.

Hands jammed in her jeans pockets, she watched the horse frenziedly paw the sawdust. She was so preoccupied that she almost didn't see the discarded bit of plastic. Then Death Threat nearly trampled it before she was able to retrieve it.

For a moment she stared uncomprehendingly at the thing in her hand: a small plastic syringe. The kind used for administering medicine. She lifted it to her face and inhaled. She recognized the faint odor. Retlin. It was an amphetamine that acted differently on different horses. But why was Death Threat being given Retlin?

Unless...

Somehow she made it through that day's scenes with Death Threat. She had missed Jed's reassuring wink, although Jack had done his best to get the scenes with Death Threat done quickly. The beast had performed exactly as required, snorting and pawing and behaving abominably. Despite his frenzied state, he had managed to throw her only once, and she'd been prepared enough to make a rolling landing.

Although the first scene of the next day's shooting wasn't until three in the afternoon, she rose before sunup, well ahead of the rest of the ranch hands, and made her way to the barn in the predawn darkness.

At her entrance, a barn owl hooted indignantly, then erupted from its nesting place with a noisy fluttering of wings and swooped outside. The horses, curious, peered from their stalls to watch her. Death Threat eyed her almost placidly.

She found a hiding place behind a wall of stacked hay bales. The barn's occupants settled down once more, and only the occasional chirping of the swallows was heard. Presently she detected the shuffling of boots. Hay tickled her nose, making her want to sneeze as, cautiously, she edged her head around the bales and glimpsed a cowboy.

Doyle Reese.

He had a right to be there, of course, as long as Maxwell-Metro Productions was paying to have Death Threat stabled in one of Mescalero's stalls. So why was he moving so stealthily, continually glancing over his shoulder? Then she knew. Or, more accurately, her suspicions were confirmed.

She watched him take a vial and a large hypodermic needle from his vest pocket. When he entered the stall, Death Threat shied away and nickered nervously. "Time for our daily medicine, ol' boy," Doyle said. "Don't go giving me any trouble. Two weeks off the stuff and you forget you're a rogue horse, don't you?"

A quiet rage poured through her. "Want to tell me what you're doing, Reese?" she asked, stepping from behind the bales.

Doyle jumped. "How about you telling me just what *you're* doing, snooping around like this!"

"Following a hunch. I think you're giving Death Threat a daily dosage of Retlin—causing him to turn killer-wild."

A slow grin curved his sullen mouth. "So? The horse belongs to me."

"You could kill him, you bastard!"

His lips curled in a sneer. "He ain't dead, is he?"

"The drug can build up inside an animal. It could cause him to die later of heart failure, or a broken blood vessel."

"Well, that's later, and the filming is now, and the horse is mine. Once I get paid, I don't care if the slug drops dead in his tracks."

She stared at him incredulously. "Why? Money can't be so important that you'd do something like this!"

He glowered at her. "It is when you don't have it. But how would you know? You're a Malcolm. With money. And part of Reese land!"

She made a decision and swung away.

"Hey, where are you going?"

She kept walking, but she heard him running to catch up with her. She didn't even glance at him.

A sleepy Rand, still buckling his belt, stepped down off the veranda to head for the barn. "Mornin' Rob," he drawled. Then he noticed Reese huffing at her side. "Hey, Rob, you're bringing in cow manure with you. Better shake it off."

Reese spit on the veranda planks. "You better watch your mouth, cowboy."

She found Peter Maxwell just sitting down at the breakfast table. Despite the early hour, he was freshly shaved and impeccably dressed. She glanced meaningfully at Haydee and Shyloh, who were carrying plates in from the kitchen. They left, and she said, "Mr. Maxwell, I need to talk to you."

He took a swallow of coffee and dabbed fastidiously at his silver mustache with his napkin before answering. "Yes, Miss Malcolm?"

In terse words she revealed what she had discovered, while Reese hulked over the far end of the table, watching tensely.

"I see," Peter Maxwell said. He studied the well-manicured nails of one hand, then said casually, "Miss Malcolm, I don't give a damn about whether that animal is drugged or not. As long as the picture comes in on budget, fine."

For a moment she was dumbfounded. "You can't mean that," she blurted.

"Oh, but I can," he said smoothly. "You're not thinking very cleverly, Miss Malcolm. If filming gets shut down, Jed doesn't get his picture made, you don't get paid, and—" he paused for emphasis "—and you can imagine what a scandal would do to Mescalero's auxiliary enterprises. Its guest-ranch operation would suffer enormous losses. Besides, what are you going to do, call the sheriff—Cal Reese?"

She saw his point. She was beginning to learn about Peter Maxwell's kind. They knew about bank statements, interest rates and bribing the right bureaucrats.

At her silence, he patted her arm. "Now listen. All you have to do is keep quite about the injections until the filming is over. That's not so much to ask, is it? That way, everyone will go away happy."

She stared at him while a multitude of conflicting emotions hammered at her. Before Jed had come into her life, things had been simple, with everything black or white, yes or no, right or wrong. Now, to do what seemed right meant not only losing her own dream but hurting others... Jed, Tom and Marianna.

When she still didn't answer, Peter Maxwell rose, laying his napkin beside his plate, and said unctuously, "I knew you'd see it my way, Miss Malcolm."

He turned an annoyed glance on Doyle Reese, who was wearing a smug look. "For God's sake, Reese, be careful, will you?" Then he left, and Reese was right behind him.

Long after they had gone, Rob still stood there, turning the alternatives over in her mind.

"You ready, girl?" The words came as raspy whisper from a throat that had been seared by years of swilling everything from vanilla to mescal to cough syrup.

"Ready," Rob whispered back.

Red Eye nodded. Burlap sacks in hand, he entered Death Threat's stall. The horse began to neigh nervously. The drug had worn off a bit, and he only pranced in agitation in the far corner.

"We get caught," the old man muttered, "me one damn fine dead Indian."

Rob grabbed the horse's halter. "You're about dead anyway, from all that booze you consume."

"White kids! No respect for ancient ones." He hunkered his bony frame down on one knee beside the horse. "Hold it still, girl."

Death Threat was in no mood to be subdued, and he shook his head and flashed his hooves. She twisted his ear, and he calmed down immediately, though his eyes were still wild. "Thought you'd see it my way," she said. "You're gonna end up in the dog-food factory yet."

Red Eye caught one renegade hoof and quickly slipped a burlap bag over it, securing it with rawhide strips. After the other three hooves were likewise muffled, he rose on creaking bones. "*Vamanos*, girl."

They rode out into the deep night, Rob astride a recalcitrant Death Threat, and Red Eye on one of the ranch's working horses, its hooves also sacked. The moon was rising, enormous and blood red. A hunter's moon, she noted. The creaking of saddle leather, the clink of spurs and bits and the crunch of hooves against sand were the only sounds in the vast desert. Those and the occasional lonely yip of a coyote, who followed them with his yellow eyes.

She was reminded of Jed, not that he was ever far from her thoughts. A great sadness eddied through her like a cold morning fog. She was losing him, stealing Death Threat like this. When filming shut down, he would soon learn that she was responsible for ending his dream.

But if she'd learned anything from all the hurt and wanting and anguish, it was that she couldn't be anyone but herself. She couldn't change, not even for Jed. She had been a prize fool to think she could.

"Where are we headed?" she asked, not really caring. She couldn't find it in her to care about much of anything. Certainly not about this mule-headed horse's future.

"Where they never find horse unless we want them to. On Mescalero Reservation. Way back in canyon."

When she saw the canyon by dawn's first light—and saw what was going on inside it—she had to chuckle, even though she felt far from lighthearted. Indian bucks dressed in jeans and windbreakers were working feverishly around a large fire.

"I should have known, you old swillbelly," she said to Red Eye. "A *tiswin* still! Leave it to you to head straight for the nearest corn liquor."

Chapter 16

For the first time in years, Rob overslept. It was half past eight. She felt bone-weary, groggy. As if she had slept too long. Which wasn't the case, since she hadn't returned to the ranch until almost four this morning, just before the big house started coming to life.

"Why didn't you wake me up?" she asked Shyloh, who shoved a cup of coffee at her.

"Mom said to let you sleep, that you needed it."

Rob wondered if Marianna knew what was going on. If she didn't, she soon would.

"While you were sleeping, Rob, you missed all the commotion."

Rob turned around to where Shyloh stood at the dishwasher, removing the clean dishes. Had Death Threat been missed already? First call had been at six this morning, with Death Threat's scene to be shot just before lunch. Soon someone was going to miss the horse. When Reese didn't find the animal in the stall or out on location, all hell was going to erupt. "What commotion?"

Shyloh's grin was as delicious as if she were a cat finishing off a dish of cream. "Haydee and Rand."

"Haydee and Rand what?"

"They announced this morning that they're engaged. Can you imagine that!"

"Seems true love is budding everywhere," she grumbled. Her gruff behavior concealed her heartbreak. She would positively hate herself if she gave in and wept. It didn't make any difference that her heart felt heavy, that her throat ached from swallowing unshed tears and that she would never know happiness again. Despair, she decided, hurt worst than any physical pain.

"You look like you're in mourning," Shyloh said. "Back wearing your old clothes and all."

Maybe I am, Rob thought. She had donned her baggy overalls this morning, along with her heavy boots. Her hair was pulled back in its unbecoming braid. She was what she was. The Malcolm girl. And she couldn't be anything else. Not for anybody!

She swallowed a silly sob that threatened to escape her tightly pressed lips and blinked her eyes. They were dry and raspy. From looking through rose-colored glasses, she thought, her derision aimed solely at herself.

"Looks like some of the crew's returning early," Shyloh said, going to stare out the kitchen screen door.

"Trouble's already here," Rob muttered, and downed the last of her coffee.

"What?"

"Nothing, Buffalo Gal."

Shyloh scowled. "Don't call me that."

Rob rose and, setting the cup and saucer in the large stainless-steel sink, said, "You didn't used to mind."

"Well, I'm...I'm grown up now. Except you—and Colt—don't seem to realize it."

Rob surveyed the girl, whose cheeks were the same hot pink as the dish towel she was holding. "I think I see. Yes, you are. You're right—I should be calling you Shyloh. You're a young woman now."

And facing all the joy and heartbreak that come with womanhood.

Rob swung away, heading for the veranda. She might as well meet Peter Maxwell out in the open, her kind of dueling ground.

His rented Lincoln halted in the yard. Before the chauffeur could even open the door, the producer was out of the limo and stalking toward the veranda. She jammed her hands in her pockets. "You wanted to talk to me, Maxwell?" she asked offhandedly.

"Damn right I do!" He planted his fists on his hips, shoving back the front flaps of his jacket. He glared up at her, the veins in his temples beating a furious tattoo. "You get that horse back in that stall today or

I'll have Sheriff Reese down on you so fast your head will spin!''

"I don't know what you're talking about, Maxwell.''

Beyond him, another car was pulling into the yard. A red Porsche. The ache in her heart rose into her throat so quickly that it almost choked her. Jed climbed out and strode toward them. He was so ruggedly handsome, so totally male, that she nearly sagged against the veranda's cedar post. He looked just the same, with the same disheveled burnt-gold hair, the same sensually chiseled mouth, the same incredible amber eyes that could peer right through to her soul. At the moment those eyes looked tired, his face fatigued, as if he had been driving all night.

Peter Maxwell followed her gaze. "You're back, Pulaski, and none too soon. Your ingenue here has made off with Death Threat.''

Jed glanced at her, taking in her braided hair and hayseed clothing. "Reese was shooting him up with a daily dosage of Retlin,'' she said wearily. "To make him wild enough for his role. If he'd continued, he might have killed him.''

"Tell her to get that horse back in his stall, Jed. Now!''

Rob closed her eyes, swallowed hard, then stared at Jed through her tears. She understood how much he wanted to make this picture, how much he loved this film. She could never let herself—not in all the lonely years to come—begrudge him his choice. She must not become a cynical, hard-bitten old maid. Her finger-nails dug into the cedar post's rough bark.

Jed shrugged. "She's her own woman, aren't you, sweetheart?"

She stared at that hard, handsome face, searching for some trace of mockery. But there was none.

"Pulaski!" Maxwell shouted, losing his cool, un-ruffled poise. "Order her to bring back the horse or I'll see to it that you never make another picture. No backer or distributor will want to touch you after I've finished with you."

Part of her fascination with Jed had been his un-compromising courage. Now he stood to lose every-thing, but he only gave the producer one of his grim smiles. "No one has ever tamed Rob into doing what she doesn't want to, and I'm certainly not going to try now."

"Do you believe it's really haunted?"

Rob switched off the pickup's engine and stared si-lently at the dilapidated line shack, shed and corrals at the base of Slaughter Mesa. A harsh heat lay over the baked adobe and dull sagebrush. Not very promising. Others wouldn't see the barren beauty of this part of the land, her part of Mescalero. It was a sweeping canvas of breathtaking sunrises and sunsets, serrated mountains and whispering golden sand fused into glass by the explosion of the first atom bomb.

She leaned her forearms on the steering wheel. "I don't know, Jed. As a girl, I spent a lot of anxious hours prowling these ruins. I was hoping and praying I'd get a glimpse of Grandma Ellie's restless spirit, and at the same time scared to death that I really would."

Jed shifted in the pickup to face her. He grazed her neck with his scarred knuckles. "Tell me their story. Red Eye and your grandmother's."

Sensuous shivers curled through her stomach. "Years ago, as a young man, Red Eye was a renegade," she said huskily, feeling the pleasurable sensations all the way to her toes. "When this part of the country was still largely unsettled, and the only law was a man's gun.

"Anyway, he used to smuggle contraband liquor across the Mexican border during Prohibition. He used the Mescalero line shack to hide out in, and one day Grandma Ellie found him there, wounded. Don't think about him as he is now, Jed, but imagine him then, as a young man. Strong and fierce and handsome."

"Was your grandmother already married?"

"Yes. Even though she was young, maybe no more than seventeen, she already had a son, my father— Robert. Hers was one of those marriages made for the convenience of both parties—my grandfather needed a wife, Grandma Ellie needed a man to help her run Mescalero. The ranch wasn't nearly as big then as it is now, but she still needed help. She truly cared for my grandfather, I think. But that couldn't stop the wild passion she felt for Red Eye."

He glanced out over the silent buildings. "And this was their trysting place, where they came to pour out their passion?"

"Yes, I suppose you could call it that. After Grandpa died, she ran the ranch almost single-handedly. She was nearly forty or thereabouts. Red Eye came and went when the notion struck him. He wasn't the kind to be halterbroken. Grandma understood that. But when she took sick in her old age, he turned his back on the lure of the wild country and up and moved in with us. Didn't even bother to ask our permission."

Jed chuckled low. "Red Eye wouldn't."

"He's been at Mescalero ever since—except for a spell after she died. Like a lone wolf, he took off for somewhere. He never did tell anyone where. But I have the feeling he came here to live with his memories."

"Or maybe to find her tormented ghost, searching for the lover she couldn't have in life?"

Rob shivered again, not so much from Jed's gentle stroking of her nape as from the feeling that maybe there *was* a spirit world. The Indians certainly believed it. Believed that the dead returned as clouds—in summer rain, in winter snow. Maybe Red Eye believed it enough to will it to be so.

"I never had the courage to ask him," she said in a whisper. "He's too private. After I grew up, I told myself that it was just a story spread by superstitious people. At that time I couldn't believe in a love so strong that it could conquer time and space."

Biting her lip thoughtfully, she glanced at Jed. "Now I'm not so sure. I've learned a lot this summer about the power of love."

Jed cupped her neck and drew her face toward his. His lips barely brushed hers in a kiss that was more an exchange of breath. "I've been the one to learn, Rob. To learn that people are more important than achievements."

She laid her head against his shoulder. "What happens if *Sierra Sundown* winds up half finished and on the shelf?"

He nuzzled her neck. "No way, sweetheart. Maxwell will come to his senses first. He can't afford to have a scandal tarnish his immaculate image. He's already hinting at playing ball your way, with Death Threat in your care. I even suggested that the film company purchase the stallion from Reese, and when Maxwell telephones his numbers people in the L.A. business department, I'll bet they'll see it that way, too."

"And Reese?"

"That creep will be only too happy for the money, but, knowing Maxwell, Reese is going to come out on the short end of the deal."

That pleased her. Still . . . She turned in Jed's embrace to face him. She had to see his expression. "Jed, what will happen to us? What are we going to do?"

He cupped her face, his fingers splaying into her unbound hair so that it cascaded over his hand. "Fol-

low your grandmother and Red Eye's example. Make
our love where we find it.''

His tongue tantalizingly traced the curve of her
lower lip. "I thought we could start right here at Mescalero. Film their love story. It would take me a year
at least, to write the screenplay, get financing, all that
stuff."

Hollywood people didn't hold to old-fashioned
traditions like marriage, so this was the hardest thing
in the world for her to say, but she had to do it. "Jed,
I'm pregnant." Her lips barely moved.

His fingers drifted down to unbutton her shirt and
to boldly graze one overfull breast. Waves of silky
pleasure washed through her. His mesmerizing voice
was little more than a breath. "I already guessed,
sweetheart."

Her eyes widened. "How?"

His grin was archly male. "This lovely bud is no
longer a dusky pink but a rosy brown." His fingers
lazily plucked her rapidly hardening nipple, but his
next words weren't so supremely confident. "I suppose you understand that this kid of ours is going to
be a Polish Pulaski and not a Mescalero Malcolm?"

She smiled docilely—or, at least, she tried to.
"Whatever you say."

"Well," he said, nibbling at her ear, "I had also
planned to say something about the subject of Oscar
Wilde."

"Oscar Wilde? Now?" Jed was practically pushing
her down onto the seat.

He chuckled, his laughter tickling her ear. "Now's the perfect time, sweetheart. As our friend Oscar said, 'I have the simplest of tastes. I am always satisfied with the best.'"

* * * * *

Silhouette Intimate Moments

COMING NEXT MONTH

#257 BUT THAT WAS YESTERDAY—Kathleen Eagle

Sage Parker had a busy life on the reservation, rebuilding his ranch and struggling to teach his people the value of the old tribal ways. Then Megan McBride became his boss and turned his familiar world upside down. She was everything a woman could be, and before Sage could back away, he realized she was also the only thing he needed.

#258 CODY DANIELS' RETURN—Marilyn Pappano

Border Patrol agent Cody Daniels had never wanted to see Mariah Butler again, but when she became a suspect in his latest investigation, all his old feelings for her resurfaced. His sense of duty wouldn't let him clear her without question, but his heart wouldn't let him betray the woman he was beginning to love all over again.

#259 DANGEROUS CHOICES—Jeanne Stephens

Abby Hogan had believed for years that Jason Cutter was a cold, uncaring man—until her job as an insurance investigator brought them together again. Abby soon discovered that she was interested in Jason, but old habits die hard, and only a dangerous confrontation with some real villains made her realize that what she felt was love.

#260 THIS ROUGH MAGIC—Heather Graham Pozzessere

Wolves were howling and the Halloween moon was full when Carly Kiernan came to the castle and met the count, a fascinating man who dressed in black and disappeared at will. Carly knew that everything would seem different in the light of day, but the morning only brought another question: why was she falling in love with a man whose very name was a mystery?

AVAILABLE THIS MONTH:

#253 THAT MALCOLM GIRL
Parris Afton Bonds

#254 A SHIVER OF RAIN
Kay Bartlett

#255 STAIRWAY TO THE MOON
Anna James

#256 CHAIN LIGHTNING
Elizabeth Lowell

ATTRACTIVE, SPACE SAVING BOOK RACK

Display your most prized novels on this handsome and sturdy book rack. The hand-rubbed walnut finish will blend into your library decor with quiet elegance, providing a practical organizer for your favorite hard-or soft-covered books.

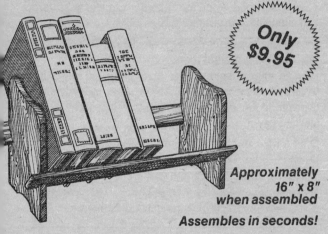

Only $9.95

Approximately 16" x 8" when assembled

Assembles in seconds!

To order, rush your name, address and zip code, along with a check or money order for $10.70* ($9.95 plus 75¢ postage and handling) payable to *Silhouette Books*.

Silhouette Books
Book Rack Offer
901 Fuhrmann Blvd.
P.O. Box 1396
Buffalo, NY 14269-1396

Offer not available in Canada.

*New York and Iowa residents add appropriate sales tax.

BKR-2A

Silhouette Intimate Moments

WHEN OPPOSITES ATTRACT

Roberta Malcolm had spent her life on the Mescalero ranch. Then Hollywood—and Jed Pulaski—came to Mescalero, and suddenly everything changed.

Jed Pulaski had never met anyone like Rob Malcolm. Her forthright manner hid a woman who was beautiful, vibrant—and completely fascinating. But Jed knew their lives were as far apart as night from day, and only an all-consuming love could bring them together, forever, in the glory of dawn.

Look for Jed and Roberta's story in *That Malcolm Girl*, IM #253, Book Two of Parris Afton Bonds's Mescalero Trilogy, available this month only from Silhouette Intimate Moments. Then watch for Book Three, *That Mescalero Man* (December 1988), to complete the trilogy.